THE BLACK FEAR

A MURDER AND GHOST MYSTERY NOVEL

POMPI MAZUMDAR

THE BLACK FEAR

(A short murder mystery)

By

Pompi Mazumdar

(Edited by Deepa Narayanan)

English is not my mother tongue, yet I tried to write this book in English as it is a global language, and the script is easily read and understood by a huge audience. Although I have endeavoured to publish the book with correct spelling and grammar, in case you find any error in this book, you are requested to bring the errors to my notice by writing to me at pompi.mazumdar@gmail.com.

Book description

"The Black Fear" is a short murder mystery novel, which centres on a couple of murders and one suicide at a home, all within twenty four hours. This story narrates the darkness of a soul, seeking vengeance in its failure to see right from the wrong, and reveals the truth and the reasons behind the brutal murders, keeping the readers engaged until the end.

I dedicate this book to

My parents, Mr. Pijush Mazumdar & Mrs. Manju Mazumdar

Grandparents (paternal) Late Mr. Prasanna Nath Mazumdar & Late Mrs. Gyanobala Nath Mazumdar; (maternal) Late Mr. Kshirodh Ch. Nath & Mrs. Sufala Nath

"God is the Creator of this Universe. We are the children of God. Our Parents are our Creator. Hence, our Parents are God. So we should always worship our Parents. We are here in this universe because they brought us here. Whatever we are today is only because of them. So we should always value them, respect them and worship them."

Pompi Mazumdar

My father and my grandfather always used a proverb, one that became one of my favourite quotes/proverbs, and has inspired me to be ambitious since my childhood.

"Uccho dikhey lokkho rakhiya charibey ek tir

Vidhiley Vidhitey parey himalayer sheer"

("Always aim high and release the arrow of your goals towards the topmost height; it might pierce everything and take you even far beyond the highest peaks of the mountains.")

"Always dream big to fly high."

Acknowledgements

I would like to thank all the situations that led me to take up writing. As people, I have noticed that most of us keep complaining to God about our small problems, always seeking His intervention in finding our solutions.

I believe that God patiently listens to us and never responds to our questions on time according to our wishes because He is the only one who understands that there is a time for everything. He prepares us in His own manner to face our circumstances and the odds in our life. And in the process, while to us, it may seem like we are struggling and failing, I believe that we are all only learning and finally finding solutions to all our questions and unresolved situations.

In my life too, there have been many ups and downs, and I kept looking for someone to blame those failures on—people and situations that may have not necessarily wanted to harm me or bring me pain. Of late, though, I have realised that whatever happens, happens for our wellbeing. Of course, I talk for myself when I state that had challenging situations not been a part of my life, I would not have been who I am today, a writer and an author.

I would like to thank God for giving me a beautiful son whose arrival gave birth to a new me and changed my entire world, for the birth of my son brought a new identity and meaning to my life.

I would like to thank all my friends, family members, colleagues, my networks, and the entire JobsForHer.Com team who always encouraged me to take up writing and appreciated my writings.

I would like to thank my husband Aniruddha Sarkar who always helped me with all the resources and opportunities I needed to grow, and helped me embrace the process of reading, writing, learning, and exploring.

I would also like to thank Wordpress.com, Linkedin.com, and Facebook.com for giving me the platforms and opportunities to showcase my skills and talents and helped me reach out to millions of readers and customers across the globe. And last but not the least, I would like to say SPECIAL THANKS to my dear friends Sangita Kumari Rath and Debasis Sahu from Bangalore, who always supported and encouraged me and appreciated my skills and stood by me through thick and thin, and especially throughout the entire process of the publication of my first book.

Roshni Roy, my neighbour from Bangalore, you are my inspiration. You came into my life as an angel and blessed me with your magical stick of wisdom. Lots of love, thanks, and wishes to you.

I also thank my editor for her thoughtful suggestions and changes.

"Every single person and situation whether good, bad, positive, negative, evil, the divine is connected to us for a beautiful reason."

&

"God always has something good in store for all of us."

—— Pompi Mazumdar

Prologue

It was a beautiful morning, and unlike the other days, there was a slight chill in the air, and the breeze that blew in through the windows brought a much-needed respite for the figure that seemed to be hunched behind the clothes rack. The activity on the trees close by and the resounding chirps of birds may have fooled anyone else but that person into thinking that the beauty of the outsides would naturally seep into the insides of the room that once used to be a cheerful boutique. Because for all the joy that radiated outside, the room was reeking of fear. A fear that comes but once in a lifetime: the fear of a violent death.

An apparition stood at the door, clothed in black from head to toe, facing the huddled figure propped against one of the lower shelves in the room, now bleeding profusely. "What began because of you shall end here with all yours," said the apparition from the door, and then pulled out an axe and plunged its blade once more, deep into the heart of the figure on the floor. The terrifying screams that escaped echoed through the room.

Then, the dark figure pulled out a gun, and without another second's delay, turned it on its head. The echo of the gun shot brought a sudden stillness that transcended to the atmosphere around, and the world suddenly came to a halt.

Chapter 1

The 100-year-old house had been locked up for many years, but it remained a cynosure of all eyes. A short gravel driveway led to the dark iron gates of the acreage, inside which the grand estate rose. Peeking out of the lush foliage in one of the pockets of the Mumbai suburbs, the façade of the double-storeyed Treehouse Estate exuded an unmistakable Victorian charm. The tall structure, with slanted roof on stonewalls and a glass-walled room with wooden beadings painted green projecting from its eastern side was an unexpected stunner located in the heart of one of the most populated suburbs in a city that was known for its capacity to fit in lives and grand dreams into matchbox spaces. Matching the frontage of the dwelling, tall stonewalls surrounded the property too, much of which was allowed to be taken over by curtain creepers and shocks of magenta bougainvillea peering through the corners of the walls.

Today, the chains securing the iron gates were unlocked, and passers-by got a satiating glimpse of the beautiful property inside. Akhil Ambani, who had returned from California to India with his beautiful bride, had bought the estate for a tidy sum, and the newlywed couple was setting up home there. It was all dream-like—right from when the couple had met a year ago at Nisha's home in Mumbai to how they had both fallen in love with the property they were now moving into.

It was not only the liveability that attracted the couple to the property but also its antiquated ambience and a history that went a long way back. Before this, the property had belonged to Siddhanth and Suchita Malhotra, and before that, to the Malhotras' parents and even before that, to their ancestors, going 100 years back when it was first constructed. Despite how old the Treehouse Estate was, or perhaps because of it, it was a sturdy, well cared for structure, with minimum required renovations having been undertaken regularly to suit the needs of the newer generations that lived in the house. It hadn't, however, been lived in for some years, and the lack of care showed in some spaces in the house.

But Nisha loved houses that had a tale to tell and the history buff in her loved to play a game in her mind, teasing out life stories of people who lived there, tales that seeped through the walls of these homes, as she believed. Moreover, Nisha had always dreamt of living in one such. And Akhil loved Nisha enough to have moved into a jungle if that's where she wanted to live. Ever since she'd learnt about the property and visited it with Akhil, she couldn't wait to live there. With the bare minimum renovations done to the place, the couple moved in lock, stock, and barrel, knowing that the rest of the renovation wouldn't affect their daily lives too much.

Akhil had only recently taken over his father's business completely, manufacturing and procuring medical equipment for the medical fraternity in India. The business was headquartered in California, with branches in Asia and the Middle East. Business was good. When he met Nisha at her home in Bombay last year, it was the first time he had travelled to the country. But he was there to meet Nisha's brother Roni, a business associate in California who was planning to set up and manage wider operations in Bombay. But on seeing Nisha, it was love at first sight for Akhil. Nisha had just walked into the study room where Akhil and Roni were talking to each other, giving instructions loudly to someone behind her, looking that way, unawares of the duo in the room. She had walked to the armchair in the corner of the room, placed right across the men, and plopped herself into it, with her long legs riding up one of the arms of the armchair and her head on the other. It had taken her a moment to notice the deathly silence that rode up from the room, and she looked up from her position to find Roni's deathly gaze at her, willing to tear her down. Then he spoke, an artificial calm penetrating his voice, an added edge of deathlike self-control seeping into it. "Er, Nisha. This is my business associate Akhil from California, who has dropped in *as I had told you he would*, to discuss our business expansions in the city," Roni said, with an extra emphasis on "as I had told you he would" hoping his muddle-headed sister would remember she was not to have entered the room!

"Oh!" Nisha said, floundering, but still on the chair, her head jutting up in a manner that could have scared any normal being with the possibilities of spondylitis. "Indeed, Roni had mentioned it to me. How stupid of me to not remember. Er... to forget, I mean. Not remember, that is," she said, first looking at Roni, who was trying even harder by the moment to control his fury at his adorable but mostly befuddled younger sister, and then looking at Akhil, almost wonder-stuck, unable to look back at Roni then. Had Roni not cleared his throat dramatically, Nisha may have continued lying in that position, with her neck pushing her head up to look at Akhil, mouthing profuse apologies about "not remembering" and "forgetting". But presently, her gaze had broken and quickly moved to her brother, whom she could see may have been enjoying imagining throwing her himself into a moat full of starving crocodiles.

She tried to smile, which unknown to her turned into a giggle instead, and even before she could control it, she was struggling unsuccessfully to get out of the armchair, the slippers she had kicked off before she plonked on the chair nowhere to be seen or felt with the one foot she could manage to get on the ground. And Akhil, with a silent gaze and warm smile playing in his eyes, had walked over towards her and offered her his arm. She stared at him and then at his outstretched arm, and as if something inside her head finally kicked into gear, she latched on to it and pulled herself off the chair. Willing herself really hard to get her gaze off Akhil, she looked back at Roni who was now all but slumped on his study chair, with his arms on the table, trying to support his head. She had run out then, instead planting her foot right on her "saviour's", which made her gasp. She considered apologising again but instead choosing damage control over anything else, she disappeared from the scene as quickly as she could!

Akhil had missed a heartbeat even as he had watched Nisha stride into the room, her silky undone shoulder-length jet-black hair falling all over her face as she plopped onto the armchair. But her soft, gaze-y muddle-headedness was what clinched it for him. He knew he was in love just as she had begun apologizing, swinging between "remember" and "forget" for as long as it took for Roni to interrupt her with the strategic clearing of his throat.

If one was to ask Nisha, though, she wouldn't be able to point out exactly what about Akhil had got her taken completely. It may have been how she had seen him looking at her lying, as awkwardly as she was on the armchair, with a glint of sparkle in his eyes and a warm smile playing upon his lips, seeming genuinely wonder-stuck at what he was witnessing. Or it could have been when he walked over to her to help her get up from the state she was in, while all her darling brother could manage was to seem embarrassed of her...er...again!

It hadn't taken long since for them to figure out that they wanted to spend their life together. She lost in her little world as long his arms were around her, and he hoping he'd never have to live without her.

It was a riverside wedding, and the ceremony was one that friends and family remembered for a long time to come. Upon seeing how much Nisha had wanted to continue living in Mumbai, between Roni and Akhil, they decided to change their initial plans, and that Akhil would stay back in Mumbai to look after the newly set up operations in the city, while Roni would continue at California to take care of the main office. Akhil could trust no one but Roni to do a fantastic job of it.

Chapter 2

Life was beautiful in Treehouse Estate. Nisha had enough to keep her occupied in and around the old house. The property came with a lawn, which she had begun taking interest in. She tended to the plants and trees growing in abundance. It was around the early summers, and the garden was flush with flowers. The fruit trees had started flowering too, promising a nice crop of sapotas and mangoes the coming year. Nisha had also taken up bringing to life back to the old, long uncared for vegetable garden in the backyard, growing her and Akhil's favourite vegetables in it.

For Nisha, mornings at the gardens began after she and Akhil had a filling breakfast of South- or North-Indian savouries and Akhil left for work. She would water the plants, diligently airing and manuring the soil that had not been turned for days, chopping away diseased leaves from plants, etc. Akhil remained busy with his office work throughout the day, sometimes even travelling for business meets, but on days he was in town, he tried to get back home early enough to spend the evening with Nisha in their well-manicured lawn.

It was a couple of months after they had moved into the house, one day, when working in the rose garden patch on the eastern side of the house that Nisha noticed the room on that side, its corrugated glass walls once again intriguing her curiosity. The room was used as a boutique by the earlier owners, Nisha had been told, and their 27-year-old daughter Simran had handled the store. Nisha had also heard that the store had to be shut down suddenly—as had the house—all wrapped up and put up for sale hurriedly. And once again, she was consumed by that slight uneasy feeling she had when she had first come to look around the house and then again when they had moved in. *What had actually happened to the family? Could the rumours she had heard be true?* Every member of the family had died while living there—she had heard it through the grapevine. Of course, no one talked about it openly, and Akhil and she found the rumours to be an amusing topic for their evening chats. But the possibility of a truth in any of it had terrified as much as fascinated the romantic in her, and kept her curiosity hooked.

Today, while turning the soil around the wild rose bushes, she decided she couldn't hold back her curiosity and ran into the main house to get the keys to the boutique. The lock on the door opened easily, and she tiptoed into the room, half fascinated, half curious. The room extended almost 8 by 6 feet. The racks that had once held all of Simran's collections when she ran the boutique were still intact. There were no clothes or any of the merchandise that may have been lined up on the racks, but just looking around made Nisha feel as if all those were once hurriedly taken down. Something about the thought, as involuntarily as it had entered her mind, nudged that vague but now familiar sense of worry in her again.

Just as she decided to lock up and get back into the main house, she thought of making another cursory check around the room. She had gotten Ramya, her 18-year-old help at home, to dust and clean up every corner of the house, including the boutique room. So she was surprised to notice thick cobwebs lining up in some of the corners of the room as well as the racks. *Why hasn't Ramya done this area, especially when I had left clear instructions around it?* Nisha thought irritably.

After locking up the room, Nisha walked out into the garden, picked up her gardening tools that she had left behind when she'd been to the room, and entered the main house. She walked into the kitchen where she knew Ramya was preparing lunch and accosted her, "Ramya, haven't you been cleaning the boutique?"

"Of course, *Di*[1], I just did that room yesterday," replied Ramya.

"Then why is it still dusty and covered with cobwebs?" asked Nisha. "Please ensure it's gone by the time you are done for the day, Ramya. You know I don't like to repeat things about work that needs to get done."

Ramya knew better than to argue with Nisha. Nisha was kind and easy to work for, never interfering with another person's work as long as the work got done. But yes, the work had to be done. And Nisha didn't expect to repeat herself to anyone, least of all her instructions. Ramya had enjoyed these months of working here, where she could organise her day according to the work she need to complete before she left for the day. And she was a hard-worker, always ensuring that she completed her work well and on time. And she knew Nisha Di liked her for that. Even in the little time she had gotten to work in Treehouse, Ramya and Nisha had grown a certain rapport. She knew she would never stop working for the family unless they moved.

So also, Ramya felt very uneasy as she heard her Di speaking to her with a tinge of harshness around her query. "But don't worry, Di; I shall clean up that room once again," she said.

"Okay," said Nisha, looking visibly cooler than she was a second ago. "But you don't have to do it today. You'd told me you needed to leave early today, didn't you? Ensure you do it tomorrow though, just before you start cleaning up the rest of the house."

Ramya agreed, but she was suddenly aware of the tightness in the pit of her stomach. She used to arrive early at Nisha's home, when the skylights were still dim and it was still twilight. The thought of entering the room that early in the day with almost no lights at least until she could switch on the lights from within made her flesh creep. Moreover, she'd heard some rumours about the place too.

Chapter 3

The next morning, Ramya arrived at work as usual, and the security guard at the gate let her in at around 5.45 a.m.; it was still dark outside. Nisha and Akhil seemed to be still asleep—the curtains in their bedroom were still drawn. Ramya entered the work-area, picked up the cleaning kit she needed to start her workday with, and headed towards the boutique across the stoned pathway of the lawn.

But as she reached the east side of the house, she could see lights in the boutique were switched on. *Did I forget to switch off the light as I left here yesterday*, Ramya wondered. But then she remembered she had not gone to the room the previous evening and Nisha Di had gone in there in the daytime, when she hadn't needed the lights on. Ramya kept walking towards the room, her limbs taut. But something stopped her in her tracks. She thought she saw a movement in the room. Now Ramya was gripped by fear. *But it could be someone from the house*, the rational part in her brain told her; she kept walking, choosing to ignore the clamping sensation in her stomach that was growing tighter by the second.

But once she reached the doors to the room, she noticed it was unlocked. She had in her hand the only key to the room. Her hands were shivering now as she pushed open the door. Just then, she heard the soft tones of wind chimes, but besides the fact that there was no breeze blowing outside, Ramya knew there were no wind chimes either. She had regularly cleaned up the barren room, and despite how the dirt and cobweb accumulated the last time she cleaned it, she never really saw any other item in the room.

Outside, it was slowly growing light. Still gripped in fear and looking around for anyone who she could call out to, Ramya slowly raised her arm to the switch board to switch off the lights that were lit, only to discover that none of the switches on the board had been in the ON position. Sweat was dripping down her forehead now, and Ramya could hardly breathe. She turned around to look back at the pathway she had taken to get here from the main house, and at a distance, where she may have been a little while ago as she headed towards the room, Ramya noticed a figure standing still. The sight kept her frozen to where she stood; but just as she turned her head to look inside the room, all she could do was let out a piercing scream that rang through the stone walls of the ancient property.

****

When Akhil and Nisha got there with the security guard, they found Ramya lying unconscious on the floor, with her head bleeding from a fresh wound that she may have got by falling backwards on the rocks that lined the entrance of the room. Her cleaning kit was lying thrown away from her. Her body was burning with fever, and there was some frothing around the corners of her mouth. The door to the room was locked, and none of the lights were burning.

Chapter 4

Leaving the house in the care of Afzal, the 60-year-old well-built guard at the gate, Akhil and Nisha jumped into their 4×4 and rushed Ramya to the Clement Healthcare Hospital, which they had dialled into, requesting for emergency consultation. Before they left, Akhil told the guard to inform Ramya's folks at home about her. As their car rolled out of the gravel path past the iron gates and drove a little over 50 meters, Nisha once again noticed the tall white gates of the house closest to theirs, on the right side of the road. Today, a slender, swarthy woman about 70 years old with long, flowing hair stood there in an ochre-coloured saree that looked like one of the famous South-Indian silks. In her hands, she held a basket with flowers in it. The looming white gate behind her gave the woman a surreal aura. She stood there, right outside the gate, staring solemnly at Nisha as their car passed by.

Nisha could see the woman through the car's side-view mirror standing right there, staring at them until the lane joined the main road 100 meters ahead. Alarm bells were going off in her head and that familiar sense of worry was slowly reappearing in her belly, and she found herself asking, "Who was that woman at the gates?" But Akhil, still distracted from the shock of all that had happened on his property just some minutes ago, kept looking behind at Ramya who was lying still in the backseat of the car looking deathly pale, praying for her bleeding to stop.

"Hmm...? What, Ishu?" he asked her, addressing her, as he gently cupped with his palm her cheek that faced him.

Nisha, who until a moment ago, had been feeling very disturbed, suddenly returned to her present when she heard Akhil call out his favourite name for her and stroke her soft cheeks. It was almost a year since they'd wedded, but she could still feel her knees grow weak when he called out to her.

"Nothing," she said shaking her head as she looked at him and smiled. And even through those stressful moments, just one look from the other seemed to solve all the ambiguities in both their hearts.

"Ramya will be fine," said Akhil with a note of optimism in his voice. "Don't worry, okay, Ishu?"

"I hope so, Akhil. She is such a young and hardworking girl. I pray nothing untoward happens to her because of whatever happened there," she replied, looking a little confused.

"She'll be fine," he repeated reassuringly, looking at her once more before returning his glance on the road.

Soon, they reached the hospital and were greeted by two emergency paramedics who transferred the still unconscious Ramya onto a stretcher. "The bleeding has not stopped still," Akhil informed the first paramedic as they rolled her into surgery.

About half hour later, when the couple was informed that the surgery was successful and there was no more danger, Akhil and Nisha decided that he should head back home and freshen up for work. Ramya would remain in the hospital, sedated for an hour or so. Nisha decided to stay on until she came around (*perhaps enquire what happened that morning*) and then take a cab to head back home.

Akhil settled the bills at the hospital and left soon after. Nisha settled into the waiting area with a cup of coffee, wishing she could be home and shower and freshen up for the day instead. An hour later, she saw Ramya's surgeon walk out. She walked towards him to find out about Ramya, praying everything was okay.

"Good to meet you, Mrs. Ambani," replied the doctor to Nisha's greetings and queries about the surgery. He seemed to be not much older than her. "Ramya is fine. And it was nice of you and your husband to have brought her in on time. She had lost a lot of blood. But she is stable now though heavily sedated as her wound had to be sutured. If you'd like to head back home and freshen up, you may."

"Thank god!" exclaimed Nisha, unable to hide the relief in her voice. "Akhil has sent out a word to her folks too, so one of them should be here soon."

"That is nice. In that case, we shall keep you informed when she wakes up or when one of her people arrives," said the surgeon reassuringly.

Nisha nodded, left Akhil and her telephone numbers by the desk in case of further emergencies, and called for a cab to get home. She was thankful to leave; hospitals left her feeling low, no matter how high-tech they were or and cheerful their ambience. To her, they were a constant reminder of the fragile unpredictability of life.

A little into the road once she was in the cab, her mobile phone rang. It was from the hospital. Ramya's dad had just reported at the reception desk about his daughter and the staff had led him to the room she had been moved to. Yes, Ramya was already looking better, Nisha was reassured. For the first time since the events of the day unfolded, Nisha was relieved. She slumped back in her seat, wishing even more eagerly than before that she was home and freshened up.

She then dialled Akhil and updated him. He was already at work. Yes, he'd had grabbed some breakfast while on his way to work. Did she have any herself?

Also, maybe once she gets home and freshens up, she should lie in for a while before starting the day, he said. Yes, quite a day, huh? She remarked, and they both laughed weakly. Speaking to Akhil had eased her nerves, as always. She ended the call and looked out of the cab window. Her cab had turned the corner into the lane of the Treehouse, now passing the grand white gates of their neighbour's home. Nisha looked up at the house, admiring the sweeping balcony on its first floor, ornate with potted syngonium and lush creepers dangling over its sidewalls.

Once at the gates of her property, Nisha paid off the cabbie and stepped out. Afzal rushed out to her from the guard room, asking, "Is she alright, Me'm Saab?"

"Yes, Afzal," she replied respectfully. "They managed to stop the bleeding, and they say she is stable. She is going to be fine."

"*Allah ka shukr hain*[2]," he said, relief flooding his compassionate face. "I was worried, Me'm Saab. I haven't heard a more piercing cry in my entire life. I wonder what caused it. She seems like such a hardworking kid. I pray Allah keeps her safe!"

Nisha gave Afzal a tired smiled and just as she was entering her compound, something made her turn around and look back up at her neighbour's balcony. And like an omen, there she was—the swarthy woman in the ochre-coloured silk saree, the pallu of the saree draped loosely around her shoulders. Nisha could feel the woman's gaze upon her, and that sensation of something untoward began to creep back into her. But she rushed in past Afzal through the gates and hurried into the house.

Chapter 5

It was almost 11.00 AM when Nisha had bathed and finished with a light breakfast of bread and eggs when her security phone line in her living room buzzed.

"Me'm Saab, there is a man here, who says he is Ramya's dad. He says he wants to meet you," Afzal said. Nisha asked for him to be let in, and walked out from her reading room into the salon where visitors were entertained.

Ramya's dad was waiting at the entrance, looking out through the window near the entrance, seemingly lost in thoughts. He was a man about Afzal's age, and just as well built. He had a clean shaven face, with combed back salt-and-pepper hair. If he belonged to the blue-collared section of society, it didn't show. There was a certain grace in the way he carried himself. He stood there with his arms folded across his chest, his legs apart at shoulder-length distance.

Nisha's greeting seemed to interrupt his thoughts and he looked up as if partly surprised. "Good morning, Nisha *ji*[3]," he said. "I am Om Prakash, Ramya's dad. I was at the hospital when they assured me that she'll be fine. They told me that had you and Akhil *ji* not taken my girl there on time, the bleeding may have caused complications. I came to let you know how grateful I am for the care you took of my daughter. I cannot thank you enough."

"Please don't thank me, Om Prakash *ji*," Nisha replied. "Ramya is a wonderful girl and has been a great help to me since we moved in. I am sorry about whatever happened to her this morning, but both Akhil and I will ensure we get to the root of the matter and care for her until she gets better. I promise."

"Thank you," said Om Prakash. "I shall be ever indebted. But for the moment, I have moved her from the hospital after she came around and they told me I could take her home. She will stay with my sister at Taloja for a few days, but obviously, she won't be able to come to work for a few days. That's also why I came to see you today—to offer my services at least until she is back on her feet."

"Oh!" exclaimed Nisha. "It's good to know she is home then. I hope she is feeling much better. But really, please don't bother yourself with her job. I shall get someone to come in for the days she is not around."

"It's going to be difficult for you to find a replacement for until then, madam," he said. "In this city, no one usually comes once they know that the work is on a temporary basis. Moreover, I am a proud man, Nisha *ji*, and I try to pay back what I owe someone. And though I do not think I can put a price on everything you did for my child today, I would like to pay off my debts in whatever ways I can. Please let me handle the jobs around here. I have previously been a cook and have taken care of homes. I shall also be handy to run your errands. I won't give you a chance to complain. I promise."

Nisha couldn't help but admire the sincerity in the man's voice. She agreed to let him fill Ramya's vacancy. He would start work in the house at the same hour Ramya did and leave after he had prepared the evening snacks and the dinner for the day. It was all agreed upon. And despite herself, Ramya began feeling at ease. *Yes, everything would be alright*, she thought, and even as she led Om Prakash into the kitchen and showed him the work area and where the groceries and cleaning equipment were stored, she couldn't wait to get on the phone and update Akhil of, what she imagined was, the good tidings.

Akhil was in a meeting when she called, and promised to call back. But by the time he managed to get back to her, it was past lunch time, and she was admiring the dishes Om Prakash had managed to conjure up and laid out on the dining table. Om Prakash had retired into the work area to have his lunch and get on with the other chores in the house. "This is incredible, Akhil," Nisha was gushing on the phone, telling him about all that had happened since she got home, especially about Om Prakash. "And he's not only made my favourite daal, with the *tadka*[4] of jeera and chopped garlic but also kofta curry—just the way I like it, with just the perfect tinge of the mint and coriander flavours. And...and the softest rotis, too. It's almost as if he can read my mind. It feels no less than a miracle, Akhil, especially given how the day started off."

Akhil laughed mirthfully. There was nothing more melodious to his ears than the easy laughter of his wife. It filled him up in ways nothing else could. And he had been especially worried since the morning when he had seen her beautiful eyebrows knot up in a tiny frown, a cloud of emotions lining up her soft face. "I am glad, Ishu," he replied. "I love you, baby. And I hope you never stop laughing."

On the other end of the line, Nisha brought the phone from her ear and looked at his number on it even as she missed a heartbeat, wishing she was holding him instead. "I love you too, Akhil. Come back home soon today, okay?" she said, speaking softly into the phone. But as she disconnected the call and looked once again at the table loaded with her favourite dishes, she realised suddenly how hungry she was. She sat down to eat, enjoying every morsel with relish.

After lunch, Nisha retired into her reading room on the first floor adjoining her bedroom, hoping to relax with a book on the couch by the French windows that opened out into the balcony. From the window, she could see the green lushness covering her beautiful garden, and bright flowers lining up on cue. It was a beautiful sunny day. Then as she gazed a little to the other side of the garden, she noticed Om Prakash standing before the glass-room. He was facing the room and in the direction of her bedroom, with his back towards the gate of the house. He was looking at the room, his face betraying no emotion, but soon he shut his eyes and began moving his lips, as if in prayer. *Poor man,* Nisha thought, that guilt building up inside her again, *he must be trying to understand what happened to his daughter.*

Nisha watched him for another moment or two before she wondered if she was infringing his privacy and settled back on her couch, getting back to the section in her book she had marked.

The rest of the day progressed uneventfully. By 5 in the late afternoon, she found Om Prakash in the kitchen again, preparing snacks for the evening. He looked up from the bowl of batter he was preparing for pakodas[5]. "*Pakodey acchhey lagte hain, na*[6]?" he asked, smiling at her as she entered the kitchen. "I am making some just in time for Akhil *ji* to get home so you can enjoy them nice and warm."

And just before Nisha could question him on how he knew about Akhil's routine, he added, "Ramya has told me about all of your timings and routines."

"*Ji, acchey lagtein hain*[7]," Nisha replied with a smile, fondly admiring the father–daughter's sincerity and diligence.

"The pakodas are ready and served with tea on the table," Om Prakash told Nisha a little later as he walked up to her in the salon, where she was seated on an armchair reading her book.

"Alright, Om Prakash. Thank you for everything, and please convey our apologies about this morning to Ramya. Let her know I'll call her soon and enquire after her," Nisha said.

"Thank you, Nisha *ji*. I shall see you in the morning," he said and left for the day.

Akhil arrived from work soon after Om Prakash left. Nisha was still engrossed in her book when he walked up to her put his arms around her from behind her. Being so caught up in her book, she was taken by surprise and she let out a scream, jumping out of the armchair but laughing out upon seeing it was only her Akhil, feeling foolish about seeming so lost.

Akhil began laughing too, and he walked up to his wife and embraced her. Then taking her face in his palms, he kissed her lightly on her forehead. "Go on, wash up and let's have tea," she told him excitedly. "There's so much I have got to tell you about today."

Akhil held his wife's face in his palms for a little longer, gazing into her eyes, with a smile playing on his lips. "Yes, my love. I'll join you soon," he said and took the stairs to the bedroom, two at a time.

Soon the two of them were sitting in the balcony that extended from the dining room, relishing the savoury treats with their perfect cups of tea. "This is wonderful," said an excited Nisha to Akhil who was looking contentedly at her. "We are lucky, aren't we, for Ramya's dad to come and pitch in even after her accident? It's not this easy in this town, you know. And he seems to be so good at his work too. He tells me that among other things he also worked as a cook before. I wouldn't doubt it after eating all that he's prepared since lunch. Am I a sloth if I am already looking forward to what's for dinner?"

"No, you are not a sloth," replied Akhil, "just an adorable glutton." Nisha couldn't help giggling like a little girl even as Akhil started laughing with her.

Chapter 6

By the looks of it, the Treehouse had woken up to a normal day today. There was no one screaming, nor anyone to rush anywhere. It was peaceful. The indigos in the dawn were leisurely giving way to the reds and whites of the urgent morning lights. And despite it being an April morning, the atmosphere was dew-laden, and the early morning lights through the trees in the property were creating pastel patterns in the air and the grass below. It would all soon melt away as the sun ascended the skies, tearing down its wrath on the earth. But for the moment, the world had a mystical charm about it.

Akhil was still asleep. But Nisha was at the French window in the bedroom admiring the day; she could see it was a beautiful neighbourhood. The quiet of the morning reminded Nisha of everything that had enamoured her about the property when she had first visited it with Akhil. She was sipping out of a cup of coffee that Om Prakash had left at the door.

And just like that the thought of Akhil made her turn around to look at his lying figure, his chest rising and falling in easy rhythms. She walked up to him on the bed. They had made love last night, and she could still feel his touch and breathe in his fragrances. It was unusually beautiful, making love to him last night, as if something had brought them even closer...as if they had found a new aspect about the other to explore, to love. As she remembered his hands running through her body last night, she felt that familiar pang of pleasure turning her into a puddle of mush, and she wanted all but to get back under the cover with him, to feel the hardness and warmth of his naked body. But it was already close to 7.00 a.m. and he had a flight to catch in a couple of hours to Kolkata. He'd be away from home for a couple of days this once. He was hoping to close a big deal in the city. "I'll spare you today, Mr. Akhil Ambani, because I know you need to conserve your energy for your big day," she whispered into his ears and chuckled. Then, she walked back to her seat at the window, admiring the morning lights.

The bedroom window faced the gardens that led to the gates of the property. A little ahead was the neighbour's residence, yet another beautiful one with high peripheral walls that couldn't still hide the lush balconies and landscaped terrace gardens that ran around the house.

And there, she noticed a movement in the balcony that faced her bedroom. Looking through the glass pane of her French window, Nisha could make out that it was the woman she had passed by in the cab yesterday. This morning, she was dressed in a white saree and her long black hair was left undone over her left shoulder, uncoiled up to her waist. She was standing with her head titled upwards, her arms outstretched downwards, and carrying something that seemed like bright-coloured flowers.

Nisha found herself drawn to watching the woman some more. Presently, she had stopped looking up, and then, facing in the direction of Nisha's home, shut her eyes. It looked like she was praying, for after a little while, she opened her eyes and dropped the flowers in her hand from her terrace towards the direction of Nisha's home, as if in some kind of offering. She then stood still by the balcony railing, looking steadily at Nisha's house.

Nisha doubted if the woman could see her from where she was inside her bedroom as there were no lights on inside. But the woman's actions and the steadfast gaze that seemed to be directed towards her home were beginning to unsettle her. *Who is that woman, and why do I feel like something about me is involved in all that she's doing,* wondered Nisha, that by now familiar sense of uneasiness she had intermittently felt especially since Ramya's incident yesterday returning to the pit of her stomach. But she decided to dismiss the feeling and head into the day. She walked over to the bed to softly nudge Akhil awake, her inexplicable fear soon being replaced by lust and a deep sense of insatiable longing.

But had she taken a peek from her windows at her own gardens as she headed to wake up Akhil and perhaps satiate her longings, she may have found her fears and feelings of uneasiness returning even faster, for at the same time that Nisha has noticed the woman on the terrace, Om Prakash was in the garden under the bedroom standing in the same posture as the woman and offering bright-coloured hyacinths at the door of the erstwhile boutique. And he was chanting something hastily with his eyes shut tightly while facing the door of the room, and the calm that showed on his face the day before was replaced with an ire that seemed to be accentuated by his brows being knitted together.

Chapter 7

With the remainder of the breakfast cleared off the table, Nisha went back to her book. Akhil had eaten and left earlier. She had stepped out into the garden to check on her plants and turn the soil in pots set on the east end. The white orchids she had planted a few months ago were growing beautifully. Then, she walked up to the patch of her garden that grew purple and pink asters, and chose a couple of stalks for her dining table.

She handed them over to Om Prakash to arrange in the vase that she had placed on the dining table, somewhere there wasn't too much or too little of the sun. "It's such a beautiful day, Om Prakash."

"It is indeed, Nisha *ji*," he said with a smile, and took the flowers from her. Then, Nisha sat down to read her book.

But barely was she into her book and she was interrupted by Om Prakash. "Nisha *ji*, I need to head out to the market to get some groceries for the week. I shall be back soon," he said.

Nisha looked up distractedly from the paragraph she was reading and as she stared back into his eyes for a moment, wondered what it was that Om Prakash had just said. "I need to head out to the market, but I shall be back soon," he repeated with an indulgent smile.

Just as Om Prakash was repeating what he'd said, the doorbell rang, distracting Nisha all over again, and she politely dismissed the help so she could attend to the door.

Nisha left her book on the armchair she had curled up into and straightened her rumpled clothes. *Where was Afzal*, she wondered. *It was his job to buzz me when someone arrived at the gates. I'll need to speak with him about this.* Nevertheless, she headed to check who was at the door.

Through the peephole, Nisha could see a woman standing at the entrance admiring the pots and plants in the area. Nisha opened the door, and a quick glance at the gate told her that Afzal was not at his post.

She still had a slight frown on her face from wondering where he was when she noticed that at the sound of the door opening, the woman had turned around towards Nisha and her face was lit with a smile.

Standing before her was an older woman about 60 years of age, with striking but soft features. She had fair, clear skin that graced her high cheek bones, and had thick salt-and-pepper hair cropped close in a pixie cut, which added to her distinguished appearance. She had worn a well-starched white kurta that had self-prints running all over them. She wore no jewellery other than the prominent diamond studs in her ears and a fine platinum chain around her neck. Complementing olive-green ankle-length trousers over a nude pair of sandals completed her look.

"Good morning," said the woman before Nisha could say anything. "My name is Sujata, and I must apologise for barging in like this without an appointment or call," she said. "I live in 'Manzil', the first bungalow you'd see down on the left of the road as you turn away from this street."

Nisha led Sujata into her home and to the living room, ushering her to the white leather sofa.

"I have been travelling for the past couple of months," Sujata was saying, glancing around the room in admiration. "I heard that this property had been bought and that someone had moved in. I got back home last night, and thought I'd just drop by for a quick hello and to check if you have settled in well or if you'd need any help. The previous owners were very close friends of ours, and we were among the first people to build homes in this part of the town. We went a long way back together."

"Please don't apologise for dropping by," replied Nisha sitting on the sofa facing Sujata. Something about this woman made it so easy for Nisha to feel warmed up to. "It's rather kind of you to have taken out the time to come by. I've been busy setting up this place and am guilty of not having taken out the time to invite anyone over to say our hellos. So I am glad you took the effort. May I bring you a cup of coffee or tea?"

"Oh don't you worry about any of those things," said Sujata. "I am an early riser and get done with my breakfast rather early. But thank you so much for offering. We shall soon get together for a meal or two. Today's visit was just to check in on you and to let you know that I am going to be here for a while; you are most welcome to drop by. Here's my number. Please call if you need anything."

"I will surely do that," replied Nisha. Then, they spent a little longer talking. Nisha talked a little about her parents who had worked and lived in California and then moved back to India, to her grandparents in Shimla. Nisha was eight years old and her brother Roni was about ten. The family had decided to move to Mumbai after her grandparents had passed on. Then, after her mother had passed away a few years ago, Nisha's dad had moved back to California where he lived with her brother who was running the operations for Akhil's company.

Sujata spoke of her daughter who lived with her but travelled often on work and was presently in Europe. She was about Nisha's age, Sujata said, maybe a little older. But she would have been happy to meet her, Sujata told Nisha.

A few minutes later, as Sujata got up to leave, she invited Nisha home, promising that she'd drop by in case she was needed for anything at all. "Just call me, and I'd be here," said the older woman, with another wink that made Nisha made laugh, simultaneously making her wonder what it was about this woman that made her feel so at ease.

"Please stay a little while longer," Nisha urged. "You just arrived."

The woman gave Nisha another bright smile and then walked towards her and gave her a warm hug. Nisha returned the hug, caught slightly off guard by the spontaneity, but suddenly aware of the warm feeling coursing through her for a person she'd just met.

"Another day, darling," Sujata replied cupping Nisha's chin in her palm. "We surely shall meet, and for much longer. I promise." Saying so, Sujata walked towards the doorway.

"I shall certainly look forward to having you back soon," replied Nisha, and then after a moment's thought, she asked. "Do you live in that beautiful property hidden behind the large wrought iron gates?"

"Yes, that's the one. You see, all of us that built homes here back then had a thing for large, expansive looking gates. The larger the gates, the more entitled we felt, I guess," said Sujata with a wink and a chuckle, which made Nisha laugh again. The gates to homes in this part of the town were indeed something Nisha had talked about when she and Akhil had first come around to check out the property.

Nisha then walked Sujata up to her car that was parked outside the gates to Treehouse, peeping into the tiny room at the gates looking for Afzal. He was still not to be seen. Sujata's driver had turned on the car ignition as he saw Sujata walk by. Sujata gave Nisha another warm hug before she said her goodbyes and got into her car. Nisha was still smiling as the car rolled out on the gravel pathway outside. She then turned around and walked back into the house, that fuzzy feeling of warmth of having met Sujata slowly settling into her being. She had liked the woman and looked forward to meeting her again. And her daughter. Maybe it was time she arranged a "know thy neighbours" get together at home, she thought. She began making a mental list of all her and Akhil's friends she hoped to invite over, but the thought of including that mystery woman from the balcony ran a tiny shiver through the back of her neck. She decided to let that feeling pass, choosing instead to focus on the pleasantness of Sujata's visit.

Shutting the gates behind her, Nisha walked back into the house with a smile on her face, not noticing, however, that Afzal was standing behind her, with a half puzzled look on his face.

Chapter 8

Nisha walked into fragrances wafting in from the kitchen. Om Prakash was at it again, cooking one of his basic recipes that always tasted magical. *When had he gotten back from his purchases?* a tiny voice in her head was insisting. But the aroma of freshly roasted spices and ground masala that was filling up the living room hit her taste buds, sending out signals of hunger into her brain. She was smiling contentedly as the whistle on the pressure cooker went off a couple of times, as she headed towards to the stairs that led to her bedroom. The sounds and fragrances in the house all brought back distant memories, some including those of her childhood days spent at her grandparents' home in Shimla.

But just then, she heard a loud noise, bringing an abrupt end to the pleasant ruminations. It has sounded like something heavy falling and it had come from inside the boutique area. The intensity of the noise made Nisha stop mid-step and she turned around to find that Om Prakash standing at the kitchen door. He seemed to have run out from his cooking, and was looking towards the direction of the erstwhile boutique too, a frown creasing his wide forehead. "So it's beginning, huh?" he said softly under his breath, only to find Nisha looking at him from the stairs, puzzled like a child.

"What's beginning, Om Prakash? What are you talking about? What was that loud noise?" she asked him, the urgency in her voice increasing by the moment.

But Om Prakash suddenly seemed shifty. "Er...nothing, Nisha *ji*. I request you to stand out of the way, please do not enter the boutique area without me," he said, and rushed out. But as he ran out, he had begun chanting what Nisha soon recognised as mantras.

Though she wanted to run after him, something else began to happen. Nisha remained rooted to the spot, unable to move. But she could feel a sense of dread seeping through her bones, taking charge of her, and she found herself screaming like a maniac. She was screaming despite herself, her eyes were suddenly looking bloodshot as if they had seen a ghost, and she screamed until Om Prakash ran back into the living room looking for her, and ran towards her, taking the stairs three at once, just in time to hold a now semi-conscious Nisha from rolling down the stairs.

As soon as he reached her, her screaming stopped, but like a battered body that remembered its wounds, she seemed to be aware of something that had happened to her without her knowing. Looking slightly disoriented, she faced Om Prakash as he was preparing to lift her, asking, "Why...what happened? What just happened to me? Where are you taking me?"

She could sense that Om Prakash was carrying her in his arms now, heading towards her bedroom. All her instincts knew that she had to scream for help.

Where was Afzal? Why didn't he come in when she screamed? But where had he been all day? And wasn't she audible? She had sounded so loud to herself, she thought. But why was she screaming? She had felt something, almost as if she'd seen something. Something smoke-like cloaked in black—black as coal. Who had she seen? Had she actually seen someone? But she even remembered thinking back then that there was no one around. No one she could see. So what made her scream? What was happening to her? But she was fast losing her consciousness even as she felt she was being laid on her bed. *Om Prakash*, she thought. *What's he doing? Help! Somebody help.* And then, she passed out.

****

She woke up to a blur and a barely audible someone's voice, calling out to her. "Nisha *ji*, are you alright?" repeated the voice, getting a little more clear each time.

Her body was feeling lethargic suddenly, as if all her energies had drained out of her. But she could now see the blur in front of her eyes clearing. Om Prakash was standing by her bed, looking over her with a tensed look on his face. "Nisha *ji*, are you alright?"

"Yes, I am," said Nisha and sat up on her bed with a start. "What happened? Who got me here?"

Om Prakash simply looked back at her blankly. And then he said, "Nisha *ji*, I was in the kitchen when I heard you cry out loudly, and I came as fast as I could. You must have dozed off while reading your book and seen a nightmare."

"What? No. It was not a nightmare," she cried out. "I saw something. After that lady...what was her name, who left here a little while ago? No. It was after that loud noise. You said something was beginning. And then you began chanting something. And...and then you ran out. I remember it all. I can still feel the terror...of something that was advancing towards me. What was it? What is happening to me? Why did you run out? Tell me. Please tell me, Om Prakash."

The man remained stoic, standing beside her bed, saying, "You seem to have had a bad dream. No one came home; I was in the kitchen preparing lunch, and you had walked up the stairs a little while ago after you had finished turning the soil in the east end of the garden and had plucked asters for the dining table."

"But I felt it. There was something coming to...coming to consume me...to kill me," she said, and upon hearing her own words, added "to kill me, as if. I mean, it felt like that. That I wouldn't be spared."

She stared at him for a few seconds as if in anticipation of him consenting to what she had felt. "That couldn't have been just a dream, could it?" she asked then.

"It must have been, Nisha *ji*," replied Om Prakash, his face betraying no emotions. "Because it has been an especially beautiful day today. Even you said so when you returned from the garden."

Nisha remembered thinking the same too, as she had looked out of her French windows this morning. It was indeed a beautiful day...but now it was tinged...with something she couldn't put her finger on.

Then, Om Prakash said, "Why don't you come down for lunch? It's close to half past two already, and you usually eat by 1.00 p.m. You must be hungry. It might make you feel better."

She nodded, and let him know that she'll be at the table in a few minutes. But even after Om Prakash left, she remained sitting on her bed. She couldn't believe she had only seen a nightmare. Everything was so vivid. She remembered that woman who had come home, the colour of her trousers, her platinum necklace, all that they spoke of, and that noise. Oh, that ghastly noise that she heard as she was headed upstairs after Sujata had left. *Sujata, yes, that's her name! Now, how would I remember something that wasn't real?* She was still deliberating as she walked down the stairs to get to the lunch table. She sat down as Om Prakash began to serve her from the dishes filled with freshly prepared food. But Nisha realised she wasn't hungry anymore. She held up her left arm to indicate that she'd serve by herself.

Om Prakash put back the spoon in the serving bowl, let her know that he'd be in the kitchen if she needed him, and left. Nisha just remained sitting at the table, unable to experience anything but the grip of the fear that had taken control of her mind. She could still feel the violence of that fear tearing at her throat. Had she actually only screamed in her dream? This was a very new feeling to Nisha—this blurring between dream and reality. And very unsettling.

When Om Prakash next came to check on the food, he found Nisha still seated, with her right arm extended as if to serve out of one of the dishes he had cooked. "Nisha *ji*," he called out politely.

"Hmm?" she replied and then realised what he may have seen of her then and quickly took a spoonful of the dish she had stretched out her arm for. But she got off the table without remembering what she had eaten or how it tasted. Then she called out to Om Prakash and said, "If you're done with the chores for the day, you may leave. I won't need you anymore today. I would like to get some rest now."

"Yes, Nisha *ji*, I also think you need some rest. You are looking rather pale and I see you have hardly eaten even your favourite dishes today. I'll wrap up and shut the door behind me and let Afzal know," he responded. But Om Prakash was talking to a zombie-looking Nisha's receding back. She was already on the last stair when he'd finished speaking.

Om Prakash stood there watching her enter the bedroom, his brows knitted and a distant gaze in his eyes.

Chapter 9

The rest of the late afternoon passed uneventfully. Om Prakash had left earlier in the day, as Nisha instructed. The house was empty, and the lamps on lawns and around the house, which were set on auto, turned on as the sun began to set. After switching on her favourite lamps in the living room, Nisha curled up in her favourite position on the armchair, still contemplating on the events of the day.

Akhil had called sometime soon after she had headed up to her room after lunch, though he had ended the call soon after, too, owing to an unexpected meeting he was called into. But he had sounded happy. The meetings had headed exactly as he had hoped they would. "I'll be home earlier than expected, sweetheart. See you tomorrow," he had said as he cut the call. Nisha had tried but couldn't get a chance to share her stories...her bizarre stories from the day. But his joy was infectious, and she couldn't wait to just have him home again.

But sitting on the armchair now, she was replaying all the emotions and feelings she had encountered that morning. She thought about how physical that dream had seemed to her. About how sore her throat felt. As if she had actually screamed. And not just in a dream. And that woman who had appeared in the "dream"! Nisha usually had vivid dreams, and she woke out of them remembering almost every aspect, every colour in them. As well as the people and characters that appeared in them. And yet, she knew that the dream she saw today was something else altogether.

That woman—Sujata—she had seemed so real. And familiar. Like she may have even known her from somewhere else.

Outside, the lights had dimmed, and the streetlamps had come on. Nisha could see Afzal was getting ready to leave, having handed over his post to his 22-year-old son Salim. The father–son duo shared a very strong bond, Nisha had noticed from the very beginning, and the son was as hard working as his dad and sincere. And just as respectful.

Nisha ate an early dinner and decided to head out for a quick drive to freshen up her mind. When her mind was clouded, Nisha always sought to "drive" it away. Driving, even around the thronging city roads, was a therapeutic pass-time to her. She changed into a pair of blue jeans and black top, and slipped her feet into her favourite pair of flat sandals. Then, car keys in hand, she stepped out. The fresh air outside was already making her feel better. Maybe she'd drive over the Bandra Sea Link, with her window rolled down, or head to the Juhu Chowpatty. No matter where she decided to head, one thing she was certain of: She was not going to let dark, inexplicable thoughts crowd her mind.

As she passed the gates, Salim smiled at her. She smiled back, enquired after him, and let him know that she'd be back in an hour. She could see him in her rear view mirror, closing the gates behind her. *He's a good boy*, she was thinking, *always upbeat and cheerful. I am sure he will make it well in life.* She was smiling now, the combination of driving around and seeing Salim's smiling face was transforming her mood into a pleasant one.

So it was just as well that she didn't notice the woman at the balcony next door looking down at the car as it sped away. A closer look would have revealed that she was chanting something. And her eyes, though they were following the car, were glazed, as if unseeing.

Chapter 10

Nisha got back home feeling much relaxed. Drives usually did that to her. The breeze in her hair, the sodium vapour street lamps that spilled their dramatic yellow on the black roads, the line of cars and jeeps rushing past her, heading to their destinations...it made her feel like she was watching the world from the outside. Like a documentary movie of life around her. They made her forget her anxieties...took her back to her the calm space in her head...brought back hope.

Bidding goodnight to Salim, she entered her home, secured it for the night, and headed up to hit the sack. Despite the blissfully beautiful drive along the Sea Link, she was tired. All she wanted was to crash now. Maybe even read a little before she crashed.

She turned the latch on the door to her bedroom and realised the lights in her bathroom were on. *Could I have left them on? Strange,*she wondered. But she went over and switched it off without thinking too much about it, latched the door shut, drew shut the thick curtains over the windows, turned on the air-conditioner to a cool 22ºC, and changed into her nightdress, securing the wardrobe behind her.

Switching on her reading light, Nisha got into bed with her book. A few sentences into the para she was on, she thought she heard someone call out her name. Nisha looked up from her book and paused for a few seconds wondering if she'd just imagined it. A few seconds later, certain it was nothing, Nisha got back to her book. But the rush of excitement through the day had drained her, and she couldn't progress much into the page she was reading, struck as she was by an urgent desire to sleep. She turned off the bedside lamp, tucked herself into her bed, and was asleep just as her head hit the pillow.

****

The clock at her bedside was showing 3.00 a.m. when Nisha heard someone whisper her name into her ears. Sleep-weary eyes strained to open upon hearing her name called out once again. Still cosy inside her bedcover, Nisha stared blankly into the pitch darkness ahead of her wondering what had woken her up. She remembered thinking someone had called out her name. Groggily, she reached out her hand to check the time on the clock, and her eyes were slowly shutting the world out again, refusing to let go the comfort of her sleep. But just then, she heard a click, which sounded like it came from the bathroom, and just like that, all the sleep escaped her and she was alert. She sat up straight on the bed, and reached out to switch on the bedside lamp. In parts curious and scared, she cautiously turned towards the direction of the bathroom where the noise came from.

"Nishshaaaaa..." she heard that whisper again, and she froze. And despite every nerve in her body forbidding her to move, Nisha put her feet on the floor, sought and put on her bedroom flip-flops, and slowly got out of the bed, walking towards the bathroom door. Even in the dim lights of the LED on the air-conditioner, she could see that the door she had securely latched before she went to bed last night was opened a crack. Her body was slowly turning taut and her heart was beginning to beat faster; nothing remained of the cosy sleep she had wanted to slip back into merely a few seconds ago.

It took Nisha all of her will power to walk towards the bathroom door. She slowly pushed open the bathroom door completely, to instinctively check if there was anyone inside, her eyes straining to see through the muddle between the darkness and the dim lights of the bedside lamp behind. She gasped at the reflection of her silhouette on the wide mirror on the bathroom wall in front of her. But upon discovering that the room was empty, she breathed a loud sigh of relief and half slumped against the bathroom door for support. Nisha was suddenly missing Akhil.

But just then, from the corner of her eye, she caught a movement on her right. There, on the frosted glass pane dividing the dry and shower areas in the bathroom, she began seeing blurry images of the boutique. And reflecting near those images on the glass pane was that dark shadow from the afternoon...from her dream (*...or was it reality...*), but there it was there, smoke-like, engulfing what seemed like a bent figure propped against one of the lower shelves in the boutique. The dark apparition then pulled out a bayonet and plunged its blade deep into the figure. The whole scene played out as if it were happening before her. Nisha remained rooted to her spot, watching in horror and unable to breathe as eerie wails began ringing through the room. At first, she spotted blood oozing from the bent down figure onto the floors of the boutique. Then it began seeping out of the glass pane in the bathroom. There was a knock on the bathroom mirror close to where she stood, and she noticed blood trickling from the mirror and into the sink below, every drop echoing in

Nisha's ears. The mirror was beginning to crack now, as if against the weight of a thumping blow to the wall it was hung on. Unable to move from the spot, Nisha stood watching as something began to break apart the glass of the mirror, as if almost tearing it from the top. And soon, a bloodied limb was beginning to appear through it, its fingers reaching out for something it could hold on to, as if trying to escape the death it was doomed to. Upon looking closely, Nisha could see it was a baby's limbs.

Now the wails of the bent figure in the glass pane were getting louder, tearing into Nisha's ears, screaming into her soul, begging for life. Nisha remained rooted to where she stood, horror-struck, with her finger nails digging into the door jamb. She couldn't breathe now. Her gaze shifted to the mirror as the thumping on the wall behind it was beginning get more rhythmic. And louder. No sound escaped her. But she remained standing there pushed against the door jamb, her eyes tearing up in terror and one hand on her throat trying to support it or coax it into screaming.

The trickle of the blood had now increased, and the walls around the mirror were now getting wet, turning bloody. Suddenly, the apparition in the glass pane showed up on the mirror, alongside the bleeding limb. It wore black, from head to toe, though a black hat covered its head up to it forehead. Nisha could only see a pair of eyes staring at her. Nisha wanted to scream, for she could see the pair of eyes was looking directly at her. The thumping noise on the walls was steadily growing louder. So were the wails. She then realised her screams were adding to it too, for despite how the apparition seemed trapped inside the mirror, she could feel it advancing towards her, and she suddenly recognised the eyes she saw in the mirror. They were Om Prakash's.

Chapter 11

And Nisha woke up, violently gasping for breath. She was lying in bed and her head was on her pillow, but the muscles around her neck and back were taut, lifted off the bed in an arch; her hands were clenching the sheets under her and she realised she was staring at the ceiling. When she had finally drawn in enough air to fill her lungs and felt her body relax, she noticed that her duvet was thrown away from her towards the bedside lamp, which had overturned and now lay on the ground beside it.

Nisha sat up on the bed, her feet resting on the rug around the bed. What had just happened? If it was merely a dream, everything in it had played out as a movie scene. Every colour vivid. Every noise—sharp, still resonating in her ears. She sat there looking up from her bed at the duvet, which remained on the ground near the overturned lamp.

Outside, the world was slowly turning light, and she could hear the chirps of the birds in her acreage. Convinced now that it was all merely a bad dream, Nisha got off the bed to pick up the fallen items off the floor. And then suddenly, there was that familiar thumping noise. Nisha froze in her spot, her right hand still stretched out to pick up the fallen lamp. *No! The dream is still playing out*, she thought miserably. Only, now she knew she was trapped in the dream. The thumping was growing louder. And just as she raised her arms to cover her ears, her body slowing slumping to the ground, she realised the noise was coming from the bedroom door. She straightened up, calmed her frayed nerves, and walked towards it to open it.

Om Prakash was standing there, his face showing no emotions. *Could I have been audible? Could he have heard what was going on inside?* Nisha thought.

If Om Prakash had had a quick glance into the room, his face didn't show it.

"I'd brought coffee twice, Nisha *ji*. But you didn't open the door. Is everything alright in here?" he asked.

Nisha all but heard anything he said, for all she could focus on were his eyes. They were exactly those she had seen in her...er...seen a little while ago, she decided.

"I am sorry, I'll be down in a minute," she said without answering his question. And saying so, she shut the door behind her, almost in his face, and stood against it for a few seconds until she could feel herself breathing normally again.

Nisha then headed towards the bathroom door, and gingerly opened it, wondering if she'd find anything in there, but the door opened easily and everything looked as it had the previous night before she had gotten into bed. The mirrors were intact, the frosted glass separating the dry and wet areas had nothing on it, and the walls looked clean. *So it was a dream*, she thought miserably. She walked up to the sink and splashed some cold water on her face. Why was she seeing such ghastly things suddenly?

Outside the bedroom door, Om Prakash stood holding the tray of coffee for a few seconds, his face expressionless, but his gaze was as if it bored through the wooden door. Then, he turned around and walked away.

Nisha stepped out of her bedroom and into her living room, still in her nightgown. It took all her willpower to mask self-control as she walked into the dining room. She could see that Om Prakash had laid out breakfast. It was an English breakfast today—toast, eggs and bacons, and coffee, with a side of fresh mango juice—her favourite kinds. But unlike every morning when she usually got to the dining table starving, scanning for her favourites, today she was preoccupied and hardly hungry. Outwardly in control, Nisha may have, at most, seemed distracted to an onlooker, a tiny frown playing upon her forehead. But her hands were shaking as she poured some coffee into her mug. Then coffee in hand, she stepped out through the balcony into the open air. She hadn't wanted to see Om Prakash or interact with him yet.

Outside, the sun had risen and by the looks of it, it was going to be one of those warm, humid Mumbai days. But Nisha didn't seem to be noticing any of that, for her eyes were locked in the direction of the boutique.

The nightmare. She wondered. *Could it have anything to do with the rumours I've heard about the place? The boutique? About the bodies that were found buried there?*

For the first time since she had grown fascinated about the stories and the apparent history of the house, Nisha began thinking of the rumours unromantically, wondering if any of those were true. Every occupant of the previous owners had died while living here. And while it was clear the husband and son had died in an accident, there were only speculations about how the mother and daughter had died.

Now, with her almost life-like dreams and nightmares, Nisha suddenly began wondering if she was being invited into that past. Could it have been as gory as she'd seen in her dream? With these thoughts running through her mind, she began walking towards the boutique when she detected some movement inside it. The door was open and she could see Om Prakash standing inside with his back towards it.

Braving the fears the memories of her nightmare brought back, she stepped into the boutique. Upon hearing her footsteps, Om Prakash turned around hurriedly as if caught off guard.

"How is Ramya now?" Nisha asked, trying to sound casual even as her eyes were tearing into him.

But Om Prakash just stared back at her for a few seconds, as if he hadn't understood what she had asked him. Then as if something clicked, he stuttered, "Er...yes, yes, she is doing fine...better."

Nisha simply stood there staring back at him, a trickle of courage seeping into her at noticing his discomfort. But just as she opened her mouth to ask him something else, he said, "Er...I just came to look here because...er...this is where...er...Ramya...."

Then he stopped talking and looked blankly at her for a moment, and said, "I am sorry, Nisha *ji*, but I must head back to the kitchen. And I think it's best if you leave this premise too." Saying so, he stepped out of the boutique, leaving a slightly perplexed but suddenly determined Nisha.

"No. Stop," she said, her voice now a command more than a request. "You need to explain yourself. What did you mean by that?"

"Please get back into the house before something happens," he said and simply walked back without waiting for her to react.

And despite her knowing that she needed to "react" to the tone of the voice he used just then, when he said that to her, she turned around instinctively to look at the balcony of the house next door. And there, like an omen, stood the woman in a lemon-green-coloured saree, looking back at her. The woman turned around and walked back inside her house when she caught Nisha look up at her.

And that fear began settling into Nisha's heart again, the one she had felt when she had woken up this morning.

Chapter 12

Nisha walked back into the house, her mug of coffee cold in her hand. She was suddenly feeling lost and lonely, and missing Akhil more than ever before. She couldn't wait for him to get back home.

She left her mug on the table and was contemplating on climbing back into bed when she heard Om Prakash's voice. "Nisha *ji*," he said, "I am headed to the vegetable market. I shall not be long."

Saying so, Om Prakash left. Nisha remained standing at the table for a little while longer. Hadn't he been to the market just yesterday? Or did she actually only dream of it all? All the events since yesterday began playing back in her mind, confusing her, and marring her thought processes. She suddenly felt tired, and decided to sit on her favourite armchair in the living room instead of heading back to the bedroom.

She must have been on the chair for a few minutes, with her legs folded under her, when the doorbell rang. She walked up to the door and opened it to find a smiling Sujata.

It may have been early in the day for visitors, and yet Nisha was suddenly aware of an inexplicable relief washing over her. It was as if she was in the presence of a close relative or a very dear friend. And it didn't matter to her that it was just yesterday (wasn't it?) when she first laid eyes on this pleasant woman smiling at her door, waiting to be welcomed into the house.

"Hey!" Sujata exclaimed, but her smile was suddenly replaced by a look of worry on her face. "What's the matter, Nisha? You look exhausted. Is everything alright? I was on my morning walk and though I realised it would be rude to drop in unannounced, I just had this urge to stop by to check in on you and say hello. And boy, am I glad I did!"

Nisha was trying to smile but something in her was giving way and the dam of fear and the bizarreness of all that had been happening since yesterday broke through and she found herself sobbing in Sujata's arms. Sujata let Nisha put her head on her shoulder, and with her arms wrapped around the visibly stricken woman, she led her into the living room. There she sat her down on the lounger sofa, helping her stretch her legs out and lie down with a bolster from the armchair to prop her head.

"Are you okay, child?" Sujata asked tenderly to a sobbing Nisha, who was trying to get herself together. "You were looking so happy and cheerful just yesterday. What turned around in just a day?"

Just then, Nisha could hear the tinkling of vessels from inside the kitchen. *Om Prakash must have returned*, she thought. She cleared her face, pulled herself together, and spoke aloud so he could hear her. "I am so sorry for forgetting my manners," Nisha managed to say, her emotions now almost under control. "Would you care for some tea or coffee?"

But Sujata just shook her head. "Are you alright? Is everything alright with you? Between you and your husband? Where is her?" she asked.

"Yes, yes," Nisha replied apologetically. "Everything is just fine. Akhil would be returning home in some time. I am sorry about what just happened, but I wish I haven't been strung up since yesterday, and I guess it just all burst out at one when I saw your kind smile."

Sujata smiled in response.

Then suddenly like an afterthought, Nisha asked Sujata, "You say you've lived here for many years and knew the previous owners too. Would you know anything about...er... them?"

Sujata suddenly seemed to look much older, and now her eyes were reflecting what may have been a painful memory. But before she could say anything, there was a loud crash that came from the bedroom, and Nisha sat up on the sofa, her face turning up to look in the direction of the bedroom, her body taut. Om Prakash had dropped what he was doing in the kitchen and run out too, his gaze fixed at the room. Nisha began running up the flight of stairs. Before he could even react, she was in the room. Sujata had followed her too. And suddenly, the bedroom door shut behind her.

****

There was just Nisha and Sujata in the room now, but Nisha was staring ahead at the floor where one of her old suitcases lay open, fallen from one of the top shelves, with everything inside it now all over the floor. Her wardrobe's sliding doors seemed to have slid open, and all her and Akhil's clothes that were neatly ironed and folded in place were now lying strewn all over the floor. Nisha was still staring in disbelief at the floor when she heard loud banging noises on the door, and someone wrestling with the door knob trying to open it. "Unlock the door and let me in," the voice screamed. She knew it was Om Prakash's voice.

But Nisha couldn't move. She was staring in disbelief at her bed, the heavy teak furniture, which was now moving towards her at high speed. An axe had just flown in through the French windows in the room, crashing its glass to smithereens. Panicking, she ran towards the bedroom door, twisting the door knob this way and that, trying to open it. But she suddenly remembered Sujata when heard her screaming next to her. "No, not her; you cannot take her. I wouldn't let you. No, not her. Not her," she cried.

But before she could turn her towards the older woman, or try to understand what she was saying, Nisha noticed the ceramic lamp, which she had replaced on the bedside stool from the floor where it had fallen this morning, was hurling towards her. She ducked, and the lamp crashed on the wall next to her. Shards of clay and glass from the lamp jabbed into the skin of her naked arm. She screamed at the unexpected pain it ran through her. Now, the right arm where the shards had torn her skin was bleeding.

The door was still not giving in, but Nisha could hear Om Prakash outside the door, banging at it, shouting and asking her to open the door. Nisha simply stood frozen to the spot, petrified, holding her bleeding arm. And then just like that, the door unlocked and flung open and Nisha saw Om Prakash looking determined and walking in towards her. And that's when she passed out.

Chapter 13

Nisha woke up on her bed. Blurry images soon cleared up and she found Om Prakash standing beside her, looking down at her, his arms crossed across his chest and his forehead marked with a deep frown. She suddenly remembered all that had just happened, and upon seeing him so close to her, she screamed and scrambled up to the head of the bed in an attempt to get away from him.

But a soft hand held her back from the other side.

"Please don't worry," said a voice reassuringly. Nisha felt a slight sense of comfort to know that Sujata was still around and turned to look at her.

But when she turned around, she noticed it was not Sujata; instead, she found the woman from next door in her lemon-green saree, sitting by her side on the bed. She had a piece of cloth dripping water, which she was wringing into a little mug.

"What's happening here?" Nisha cried, rattling away. "Where's Akhil? I want my husband. Who are you? Why are you in my house? Who let you in? Om Prakash let you in, didn't he? Oh I know he's trying to do something to me. I know that. I saw him."

"I am Poornima, your next-door neighbour," the woman replied. "I got here when Om Prakash called me."

But Nisha was not listening to any of that. Her gaze had turned towards Om Prakash, scathing with accusations. She began screaming, unable to control her tears that were rushing out. "That was you, wasn't it? The black shadow that attacked me yesterday on the stairs? But you tried to make me think I was dreaming then. You were playing with my mind, so I could start believing that there was something wrong with me. But I know it was you. Because...because," she said, hesitating a little, feeling a little confused. "I saw your eyes in that...er...dream—the nightmare I had this morning. What have you done? Who have you killed? Why? What do you want to do to me? Are you going to kill me too? Why?"

"Calm down, child," she heard the voice of the woman again.

Nisha was sobbing uncontrollably now, in fits, with her head in the pillow. She was scared for her life, feeling helpless, not knowing what to do or where to go. She missed Akhil and wanted him next to her. She wondered when he'd get back home. When everything would be normal again.

She could feel her head throbbing; her right arm was hurting too, each wound on it throbbing angrily. She just wanted all of this to end. She wanted Akhil. She wanted Roni. She knew she was going to die. All she wanted was to live a quiet life. Then she blacked out again.

****

It was about 5.00 PM when Akhil got back home. He used his keys to enter. Everything was quiet, and Nisha, who was usually the one to greet him at the door with a kiss, was nowhere to be seen. He called out to her but got no response.

Worried, he gingerly walked up to the bedroom, his stomach in knots, looking all around the house for tell-tales signs of trouble, if any. Once at the door, he opened it only to be greeted by the broken pieces of the lamp on the floor and the strewn clothes. Nisha was on the bed, her eyes shut. Next to her near the bed, on a chair that was dragged towards it, was seated the woman he recognised as his next-door neighbour. They had hardly even greeted each other, let alone shared pleasantries, and Akhil was suddenly suspicious of why she was there and what she was doing to his wife. He ran towards his wife, trying to shake her awake, even as he asked the seated woman, "Who are you? What have you done to my wife?"

But Nisha seemed drugged, her weary eyes unrelenting of the drowsiness in them, unable to notice Akhil's presence in the house. Now Akhil was really worried, a slight guilt rising within about how he had let her down by not being around when she may have been at her most vulnerable state. He remembered how she had sounded slightly low when she spoke with him while he was away. Could she have been trying to convey something to him? But he was so engrossed in the happy news he had to tell her it simply hadn't occurred to him that she could need something. His eyes began to tear up as he thought of the worst possible things that could have happened to his wife.

And then this woman...who is she? What was she doing in their house? And in their bedroom too? What had she done to Nisha?

But before he could ask her again, the woman replied. "Please do not worry. My name is Poornima, and I live next door. Om Prakash called me when Nisha fainted, and I'd arranged for my family doctor to visit. He has checked your wife and given her a sedative to help her sleep."

Akhil's head was reeling with all that seemed to be taking place, and a hundred questions were rushing to his mind, awaiting answers. Explanations. But foremost on his mind was who this woman was, who was talking to him right now. *What was she saying? And why did Om Prakash call her and not me?*

"And where is Om Prakash now?" was all he could manage to utter.

"I sent him to get some ingredients I needed for a little puja I need to do here," she replied.

Puja? What puja? Akhil was thinking.Poornima could see the confusion writ large on Akhil's face. "I can understand how scary this must be for you—to come home to strangers tending to your unconscious wife. I am sorry for barging in so, but I might be able to help you understand it all," she said, her voice calm.

"I am sorry. Did you say you live next door?" said Akhil, trying to keep his cool, trying to remember he was talking to an older woman, even if it was an uninvited stranger who was talking about his wife.

"Yes," Poornima said, standing up from the chair. "Akhil, Nisha's alright now. She'll be asleep for another hour or so. Please step out with me. I might even have answers to some of the questions running through your mind right now."

****

Akhil and Poornima walked out into the bedroom's balcony and sat sown on the cane furniture there.

"As crazy as it may sound to you, your wife has just had a supernatural experience," Poornima began.

Akhil sat there, simply staring back at her in disbelief.

"Someone or something in the bedroom tried to harm her, but Om Prakash managed to enter the room just in time," Poornima continued. "But just when he entered the room, she had blacked out. Om Prakash immediately rang me up and I rushed here. You see, it was I who had sent him here to keep your wife and you protected from the evil spirit still trapped in this house."

Supernatural experience? Evil spirit? She sent Om Prakash to work here? But isn't he Ramya's dad? Akhil was tossing those words around in his head, trying to make sense of all that he was hearing. *This is not the Dark Ages, with gods and evil spirits taking centre stage. What is this woman talking about? And...and she sent Om Prakash to work here? What does it mean? Who is she?*

"Is there an important occasion coming up for Nisha?" Poornima was asking, her voice breaking into Akhil's thoughts.

Akhil shook himself off his thoughts. "Err...important occasion? No. Nothing I can think of. We had celebrated her birthday recently. Our wedding anniversary is not for another six months. No festivals coming up either," he said conclusively.

And then he remembered a nagging question he had been meaning to ask, "Hang on a moment. You sent Om Prakash to work here? But I thought he was Ramya's dad and that he'd taken over when she fell ill. But he is not Ramya's dad or anything, is he?"

Poornima was shaking her head when a sudden a realisation hit him. Akhil looked into Poornima's eyes with his voice rising, "Christ! Was it you who caused whatever happened to that poor girl? So you could fix Om Prakash to spy for you?"

"What?" Poornima exclaimed loudly, a look of genuine surprise showing on her face. "How did you get to that conclusion?"

"Why not?" replied Akhil. His body was getting tauter as he spoke, his voice turning steel, a certain calm defiance seeping into him.

"No. No!" cried Poornima to a now completely stoic Akhil. "And now before you get all kinds of ideas in your head, please hear me out. I had arranged for Om Prakash to take up employment here, but no, he is not a spy! But Ramya...."

Hardly had she said those last words, they heard a movement from within. It was Nisha stirring awake. She was groaning. Akhil ran inside and sat next to her on the bed, putting his left arm under her head to support her as she tried to sit up.

"What happened to me? Why am I in bed? What time is it? And when did you arrive, Akhil? Why didn't you call me?" she blurted it all softly just as she began recollecting where she was.

Watching his usually cheerful wife in this state, Akhil lifted her and held her tightly against his chest, her hair covering his face as he sobbed into them.

"Who was that woman next to me?" Nisha was asking, her questions relentless, pushing herself off Akhil's chest, trying to get a look of his face. But the immediate past was quickly getting replaced in her mind. "Where is Sujata?"

"Who Sujata, baby?" asked Akhil indulgently, as he would a little child even as he was trying to control his emotions.

"That woman who lives down the road in the bungalow by the corner of the road—'Manzil'—yes, that's the name of her house," she replied. Nisha's body was beginning to relax again. "She came over yesterday after you left. Tall, beautiful; she had beautiful salt-and-pepper cropped hair. She had dropped in today also. We were talking and she said she knew the previous owners. She was about to tell me about them, but by then...." Nisha couldn't finish her sentence, for she was shutting down rapidly, the effects of the sedative or her lethargy, one of it, getting in the way again.

"Sit with me please, Akhil, and don't leave me. What happened to Sujata? She was with me here in the bedroom when...," she said as she shut her eyes and slipped into another bout of drugged sleep.

When he was sure she was back to deep sleep, Akhil slowly released her on the bed from under his arm and ensured she was tucked in comfortably. Then, he got off the bed. Poornima had also run up when she heard Nisha stir, and was now standing by the bed looking at her with a look of confusion on her face.

"Who was she talking about?" she asked.

"Someone called Sujata who lives close by. She says she had dropped in yesterday after I had left, and I think she was with her today this evening and with her in the bedroom," he said looking slightly confused.

"This evening, and with her here?" asked a now surprised-looking Poornima. "But there wasn't anyone else home. Only Om Prakash. I know because one of Om Prakash's jobs was to let me know about who visited Nisha."

Chapter 14

Akhil didn't know what to make of all that was going on in his house. His wife was on their bed, passed out; the room was in disarray, with most of their wardrobe on the floor. A stranger was sitting at his bed tending to his wife, and she was trying to convince him about the possibilities of supernatural experiences; and Om Prakash was a spy who kept the stranger informed about everything that happened in the house!

He walked up to the nearest chair and sat in it, as if collapsing, with his face held in his palms. Just then, the doorbell rang. A weary Akhil got up and went down to open it. It was Om Prakash. And like a flash, Akhil was taken over by a myriad of emotions and questions, and an uncontrollable urge to hit the man.

Om Prakash was caught off guard when Akhil's rock-like jab hit his nose. The former reeled under the blow, losing balance and falling on the granite of the entrance near the door, almost hitting his head on one of the huge pots there.

"Who are you?" Akhil was shouting. "What have you done to my wife? And to Ramya? How dare you work in our house and spy on us?"

The loud noises from below brought a frantic Poornima running to the door too. Upon seeing a seething Akhil lunging at Om Prakash, she ran and held his arm. "Akhil, please stop. I told you; none of this is Om Prakash's fault. He was just doing what I had asked him to do because I was worried for your and your wife's safety," she cried.

But Poornima noticed that she was talking to a man who had completely transformed from the suspicious but well-behaved man in the bedroom to a distrustful and dangerous man ready to avenge his loved one at any cost. And he had aimed at his wrath at Om Prakash, the man he thought he had employed in his house.

All that commotion had brought even Afzal running to the door from the gate. With his initial need to hit Om Prakash sated, Akhil began to calm down. Presently, Poornima and Afzal were near Om Prakash, trying to prop him up when Akhil, remembering his manners, walked up to Om Prakash and stretched out his hands for him to grab on to and stand up.

Akhil looked at a confused Afzal staring at him, and assured him with a nod of his head that everything was okay. A slightly disturbed-looking Afzal then walked back to the gate.

Meanwhile, the trio stepped into the house again. Akhil and Poornima were sitting in the living room while Om Prakash stood nearby, trying to block the blood flow from his wounded nose using an ice bag. Akhil pulled out his phone and dialled Ankit Saxena, the Deputy Commissioner of Police in the city, to report about the 'break in' at home. Ankit was also a friend he knew through Roni, Nisha's brother.

Once assured that Ankit would get there soon to understand what had happened, Akhil's seething anger had relented, although he was still impatient. "I want to understand all of this from the beginning," he said, and then staring right into Om Prakash's eyes with a rage that he didn't care to hide at all, he added, "and you better not leave out any detail."

The shock of all that happened a little while ago had worn out now, and Om Prakash was his usual in-control self. But before he could answer, Poornima began, "Akhil."

"No," Akhil interrupted her. "I don't mean to be rude, Poornima *ji*, but I would really appreciate if I heard it from him."

It was Akhil's way of ascertaining consistency in both their versions, what little he had heard of it until now. He knew that Poornima and Om Prakash had had no time to interact since she had first begun explaining the situation to him.

"Akhil *ji*, I have nothing to hide from you. But before any of that, I apologize for the cover and secrecy. And I am sorry it had to unveil to you in these circumstances. Poornima *ji* and I were hoping that we could avert all of this that happened today. Clearly, the spirit is stronger than we had imagined," Om Prakash said, and looked at Poornima who looked back at him and then began looking down and shaking her head slowly. Akhil just remained looking at both of them, feeling just as confused, with just as many questions now as he had before Om Prakash had started the 'explanation'.

"I am an astrologer," continued Om Prakash. "Poornima *ji* here is what we call a natural medium."

Poornima took the liberty to interrupt Om Prakash to explain. "When he says 'natural medium' he simply means that I can foresee some events and that I can connect with souls of some of the departed."

"Yes," he continued. "Poornima *ji* was born with a gift to be able to connect with departed spirits and souls. And what she doesn't admit is that she used to be a very strong medium for a very long time, helping people like me to clear birth charts of people, which were cursed by estranged spirits from the nether land. Poornima *ji* and I have worked together previously, and we've turned around wonderful results. But she had not been active for some years now, until she heard that this property was being bought again. Since your arrival, she has been keeping a keen eye on everything that happens here. Probably because it all happened as many years ago, she believed that the spirits were not strong enough and that even keeping an eye might help avert any untoward incidents here.

"But she decided to reach out to me just in case, and going by my charts about the place, I knew something was building up here. And Ramya...well...Ramya is not related to me in that she only lives in the same neighbourhood as mine," he said and noticed both Nisha and Akhil were looking shocked.

"Her mother makes a living by doing household chores in various homes including mine. Ramya had heard about me through her mother, and she came to me wanting to learn astrology. And, oh such a good student and apprentice she turned out to be, absorbing everything I taught her, in its entirety, and so quickly.

"When Poornima *ji* reached out to me on knowing that you were buying the property, it was Ramya's idea for her to move into your home as your domestic help. Though I was not too keen on it, she convinced me that it would help her keep me informed about all that happened in the house. And against my better judgment, I gave in to her request.

"Things were progressing well and we knew things were fine until that day when Ramya collapsed. It all happened unexpectedly. And in addition to the potential dangers it seemed to be opening up, I hated it that I could be so careless about what I had exposed the poor girl to.

"That's when we knew things were not going to be as simple as we had imagined. When Ramya was admitted in the hospital, Poornima *ji* and I decided that it was time for me to move into the house. After the doctors assured me that she was out of danger, I released her from the hospital and got her mom to take her away from here, to her village, so she was away from any effects of what was happening here."

"Given that I had heard enough stories about all that had happened here long time ago, I should have come down here before I put that poor girl's life in danger. Because after Ramya's incident, I checked my charts again, and I could see that there would be an attack soon."

"What attack?" asked Akhil, looking perplexed, his exhaustion slowly reflecting in his words.

"Like the one today, Akhil *ji*," replied Om Prakash.

But despite himself, Akhil was losing patience. He wanted to scream at anyone talking about any attack, for all he wanted to do was to return to his wife, and for everything to get back to normal. So instead, he asked, "Who was the woman who came in this evening?"

But in reply, Om Prakash simply stared back at him, and then after a moment's pause said, "Woman?" He looked confused, and then he looked at Poornima. And then he said, "There was no one with Nisha *ji* all day today."

Chapter 15

No one spoke for a few seconds. They simply sat there looking at each other instead, surprised, with one of them looking genuinely shocked.

Then Akhil spoke, "No, no...you must have missed her. Nisha told me there was a woman here in the evening. And that they were talking about the previous owners.

"I mean, she even described the woman—Sujata, yes, that's the name she told me. She said she lives in 'Manzil', the bungalow by the corner of the road. And...and yes, she even remembered how she looked... cropped salt-and-pepper hair, diamond studs, and that she was with her in the bedroom," Akhil said, tired yet desperately trying to make sense of all this.

He turned to look at Poornima; the blood had drained out of her face. "Akhil, 'Manzil' was demolished for redevelopment six months ago, leaving just the tall gates in front of the property intact," she said gravely. "No one has been living there for years now."

****

It was growing dark outside. The lights in the lawn of the property had come on as had the street lamps. Om Prakash walked up to the windows in the living room and drew their shades; then, he went around turning on the lights inside the house. But Akhil noticed none of this. He was slumped in his chair, head thrown back on the chair's headrest and rubbing his weary eyes with one hand. He didn't know what was happening in his own house. He didn't know what was happening to his wife. He was tired from a fruitful but exhausting travel, and all he wanted was to get back to Nisha. And for all of this to end.

"I need to be with my wife," he said then. "Thank you, both...I guess...for being there for her, but I think it would be best if you left now. I need to relax too."

Despite everything Poornima seemed to want to tell Akhil, he could see that she knew now wasn't the time. Instead, she simply nodded in agreement and stood up to leave. "In case of anything inexplicable or untoward, please don't hesitate to call for either of us," she said. "Om Prakash would be staying with me until this passes over."

Until what passes over? The thought was screaming in Akhil's mind, but he was too tired to ask anything.

But just as Om Prakash and Poornima were turning to go, they heard Nisha's voice from above. She was coming around, and calling out to Akhil. "Akhil, are you home? Is that you?" she asked. Akhil bounded up the stairs, leaving his uninvited guest standing there, watching after him.

He opened the door and walked in towards his wife, carefully stepping over the strewn clothes on the floor. She was sitting up now, looking a lot better than she did when he had first seen her that evening even as a chill passed through him at the memory of that sight.

"Hey, baby!" he said gently and smiled, even as he said a silent prayer in gratitude at seeing her as she was just now.

He sat beside her on the bed and put his arm around her. "What happened here?" she asked him looking around the bedroom.

"Well, I am not entirely sure, but Om Prakash and the lady next door have an interesting but absurd idea," he replied with a forced chuckle in the hope of diffusing the tense situation.

Hearing Om Prakash's name brought back a flood of horrifying memories in Nisha's mind. There was something flying at her, and the bed she was now sitting on just now...hadn't it been moving at her at a speed enough to crush her against the wall? And Om Prakash was trying to enter the bedroom. And thinking of Om Prakash brought back her sinister dream from earlier last night, and she remembered seeing his eyes in it, with a menacing look in them. "Om

Prakash...he was trying to kill me," she blurted out, the urgency in her voice increasing by the moment. "He was trying to push open the door. I know. I saw him, Akhil. I was so scared. As if he wanted to kill me. And Sujata was there. She was trying to protect me.... Where's Sujata, Akhil? She was here with me. She was talking to me about her daughter and her life and about meeting soon. What happened to her? How is she doing? What's happening to me, Akhil? I am scared. Why is this happening? Please help me." And she burst out crying.

Akhil swallowed a rising lump in his throat upon watching his wife's distress. His Ishu, who brought a smile upon everyone's face around her, just by being who she was.... His kind, compassionate Ishu. Oh how he wished he could understand any of this so he could keep her safe. And then he remembered he had called Ankit, and let Nisha know about her brother's friend getting home soon to investigate. "Everything's going to be fine, Ishu, I promise. Om Prakash and Poornima *ji*, that lady from the neighbouring house, are probably still waiting downstairs. I had asked them to leave because I thought you needed some rest. But come to think of it, I'll ask them to stay until Ankit is here."

"I'll freshen up too so that I can look at Om Prakash in the eyes," Nisha said, forcing a tiny note of bravery into her voice. "Let him know I am not scared of him or any of his antics."

She pulled herself out of bed and stormed into the bathroom to wash up, leaving a startled but smiling Akhil looking at her approvingly. He was admiring his wife's tenacity to get over her fears and boundaries to understand what was happening and perhaps to bring an end to it all.

****

Om Prakash and Poornima were surprised to see Nisha walk down the stairs with Akhil right behind her. Her face had a determined look and her pride showed in her gait.

Once she got the living room, she took on the part of the hostess rather deftly. She indicated for her guests to sit down, and with Akhil beside her on the lounge sofa with an arm around her shoulder, she looked at Om Prakash after she passed a cursory glance at the woman she recognised from the house with white gates.

"Were you trying to kill me?" she asked him without preamble.

"What?? No!!" came a shocked reply. For someone who was convinced of his guilt in the matter, Nisha was suddenly unprepared for the shocked yet calm disposition of Om Prakash. And as if she didn't know what the rest of the script was to be, she looked at Akhil, her eyes betraying her confusion.

Then, Om Prakash began talking, his hands clamped before him, and shoulders slightly slumped. "Nisha *ji*," he said, hesitating slightly at how he might sound to her. "What you've been experiencing yesterday and today afternoon were supernatural encounters with a tormented and vicious, unreleased spirit."

Nisha's eyes lit up on hearing this, and when she spoke, her voice was charged with an added excitement that was missing since Akhil had found her this evening. "So I was not dreaming about any of it after all...like you were trying to make me believe." Then looking at Akhil, she continued. "I was so worried that I was beginning to see things that weren't real."

But Akhil simply nodded and drew her closer to him.

Then Nisha suddenly remembered something. "But why did you do that to me? Why would you do that to anyone? And Sujata...where is she? She was with me in the room too, when all of it was happening. I heard her screaming at someone, trying to protect me. Did she get hurt? What's happened to her?" Nisha cried out, turning around to face Akhil, Poornima, and Om Prakash one after another.

Instead, in response, the three of them just stared back at her blankly.

"That's the woman I talked to you about," said Akhil looking at Poornima. "The woman Nisha told me lives in 'Manzil'." Poornima nodded understandingly.

"You merely had a supernatural experience, Nisha *ji*. There was no one in the house then," Om Prakash reiterated, his voice soft and his face placid but showing concern. "Ever since I began working here, I always make it a point to check the entry and exit log for any unusual visitors. Today, I know Afzal has entered nothing in it. And you know how diligent he is in his duty. He wouldn't miss anyone's entry or exit. Even mine."

But Nisha was still looking suspiciously at Om Prakash, not willing yet to accept what he was telling her. "But...but...,"she began weakly, "and I meant to ask about that too...where was he in the afternoon? He was not there when she came home. I noticed his cabin was empty."

No one replied. Om Prakash just looked puzzled. Akhil was now on the edge of his seat where he had put an arm around Nisha holding her; he put in meekly to his wife, "Ishu, are you sure he was not around then?" Now Nisha was the one who seemed to look unsure, and in response, she merely stared back at Akhil wondering if she merely had an episode of hallucination.

The quiet in the room was broken by Poornima who seemed to have a sudden idea. She sat up, and turning around to look at Om Prakash, spoke hurriedly, "Om, would you please run back home and get the picture I have on my mantelpiece in the living room?"

Om Prakash nodded his head and, without another word, ran out.

But while he was gone, Nisha sat still, trying to take it all in. She tried to gather her senses and speak, but her throat felt clamped. And then, sounding completely confused, she asked, to no one in particular. "Supernatural experiences?" "But that's ridiculous, isn't it? Because those things never happen in real life, am I right?"

"Not really, *beta*," Poornima began saying, and the affection and warmth in her voice made Nisha drop her guard a little. "Hinduism believes that transmigration and reincarnation of souls take place according to one's karma. And souls who do not complete their lifecycle in one birth come back again and again in different forms to realize their unfulfilled desires. Many religions, not only Hinduism, believe that souls cannot begin their departure to the spirit world even after their death when their desires remain unfulfilled because then they are, what we natural medium call, 'earth-bound spirits'. If they are emotionally attached to something in this world—whether happily or in vengeance—they won't be able to leave here, are unable to understand their inexistence, and yet trying to follow the similar lifestyle that they were once used to. In such cases, while they might be denied life after death, they might look for sources to communicate their unfulfilled message through. The experience you had today was clearly spiritual. And going by the havoc it created for you today, it is clear that this spirit is evil."

Though she was completely drawn into everything Poornima was saying, it was all too much for Nisha. She stood up where she was seated and walked towards the French windows, staring unseeingly at the drawn curtains.

She did believe in god, had her favourites whom she prayed to, too. She had also watched a few horror movies with her brother when they were growing up, all of which she rubbished because she never understood the logic of horror and spirits. And the idea of getting scared for the thrill of it never excited her. So she had even long stopped watching any of those movies. But now she was being told that she was being attacked by an evil spirit! She didn't remember doing anything to deliberately displease anyone living, let alone an ethereal being. *And what in the name of heaven is a 'natural medium'*, she was thinking with a growing sense of irritably.

Right then, the noise of tyres grinding on the gravel outside shook her out of her thoughts. She could hear a vehicle coming to halt. Akhil got off from the sofa and walked up to open the door, and found Ankit getting off the jeep. Ankit was in his mid-30s, with a well-built physique and closely cropped hair framing his pleasant face with light greys at the temples.

Just as he was walking towards the house, a panting Om Prakash ran in through the gates and into Ankit, with a picture frame in his hand. But upon seeing Ankit, Om Prakash suddenly stopped. Ankit's face lit up in a smile; then, shaking Om Prakash's hands and hugging him warmly, he said, "*Kaise ho,* Om *ji?*[8]"

"*Main ttheek hoon. Aur aap?*[9]" Have you come here on any complaint?" he asked in response.

"Yes. Nisha is an old friend's sister, and Akhil called me urgently about some break in," he said.

Just then, Akhil stepped into the scene, asking, "You know each other?"

"Of course, Om *ji* here is only one of the best astrologers in town and he uses the science to help the police solve many cases across the country," Ankit said with a smile at Om Prakash. Saying so, Ankit and Om Prakash walked into the house talking to each other as if unawares of Akhil. Akhil simply stood by in a minor shock about what had just transpired before him, not knowing how to react or what to think! The evening couldn't get any more confusing. And that was all he seemed to be sure.

"Okay. I didn't know that," whispered Akhil sulkily as he walked into the house behind the duo.

Once inside, Ankit walked directly up to Nisha and hugged her warmly, asking after her. Om Prakash introduced Poornima as he had done before to Akhil. After all the introductions had been made and the party had settled down, it was Nisha's chance to look as confused as Akhil did a moment ago. Clearly, noting that Om Prakash was known to Ankit came as a surprise to her, just as did the knowledge that the "suspicious woman" from next door was not out to harm her.

Poornima's voice rang in through her thoughts as the older woman asked Om Prakash, "Did you get it?"

A confused Nisha was back on the sofa with Akhil, leaning into his chest with her feet tucked under her legs. Ankit sat opposite to them on the sofa next to Poornima, and Om Prakash sat on the other side of Poornima, on a dark maroon ottoman.

Om Prakash handed the frame to Poornima.

After glancing at it once, Poornima turned around to Nisha and showed it to her. "Is this the woman you saw today?" she asked.

Nisha took the picture frame from her hand and stared at it. The picture was a crowded memorabilia of happy-looking faces. Six people, including Poornima, smiled away into the camera. Behind her was a slightly paunchy, bald man, with his arms around her and his smiling, happy face rested on her shoulder, in a show of light intimacy shared only between deep friends or lovers. Besides the couple was a tall man, smiling at the camera shyly, a woman with crossed arms around her chest standing next to him. She was looking towards her right with a smile on her face. And through the sepia tinge of the old picture, Nisha could see who she was looking and smiling at. Standing towards the right of the two couples was the woman she had come to know as Sujata. Her head was slightly thrown back in a laughter that was captured by the camera midway. She had the same salt-and-pepper hair cropped close in a pixie cut, and despite the colours in the picture, Nisha could see she was wearing the same well-starched white kurta with self-prints and a complementing olive-green ankle-length trousers with a nude pair of sandals on—the same ensemble she was in when she had first visited her. *Goodness! Was that was just yesterday?* Nisha wondered in awe. Even in the picture, the woman wore no jewellery other than the diamond studs in her ears and the platinum chain. She stood ahead of a man who had his arms around her waist looking like he was going to lift her, a determined smile playing on his face.

"Yes, that's Sujata," said Nisha, her voice shaking.

Chapter 16

"I had a feeling Nisha was describing my dear friend Suchita Malhotra. She'd lived here for over 30 years with her family," Poornima was telling Akhil. "When my late husband Debraj and I had moved in next door about 30 years ago, the suburban areas in the city were still only developing, and we were among the initial set of people who had built our homes here. Suchita's husband Sidhhanth's family, going back to his granddad, had been living here for more than 50 years.

"Sidhhanth's parents had moved back to India from Switzerland, where Sidhhant's dad used to work. This house you live in today had belonged to his granddad, who had bought it from an English man.

"Both our families got along very well. We were a cosy bunch, with regular get-togethers and gatherings. You could even say that Malhotras' kids, Simran and Rishi, grew up in our home. They'd usually be at our place for at least one meal in the day. But it was after Debraj's death that Suchita and I grew much closer. That was about seventeen years ago. Suchita would regularly drop in at home to check how I was doing.

"Through all my years with Debraj—as much as I loved him and cherished every moment we spent together—I always longed to have children, something he hadn't wanted because he didn't think he'd make a good dad! Oh I'd long given up on convincing him about how wrong he was in believing that especially when I could see how beautifully he got along with both Simran and Rishi. But at some point, it stopped mattering to me that I hadn't birthed a child. The Malhotra kids had made up for that vacuum in my life and in my heart. Our house was their second home, where they even brought their dear friends. When they were little, Suchita had even taken it for granted that if the kids were not home, they were at ours.

"I particularly remember one of the kids' friends, Mehul, who was son of Jignesh Mehra. Jignesh was also a very dear friend of the Malhotra family but lived on the other side of town. He and his wife Radhika are in the picture next to Debraj and me.

"When they visited the Malhotras, it was almost a ritual for their son to join Rishi and Simran for the meal they had at my place. Mehul used to be very fond of Simran," said Poornima, smiling at the memory.

"Then the kids finished college and went their separate ways; Simran got a degree in fashion designing from NIFT in the city, and Rishi went abroad to complete his business management. He was very keen that he joined his dad's steel manufacturing and real estate businesses. He got back in 1998. Mehul got into a college in the States, and though his parents visited Suchita and Sidhhanth, my contacts with the Mehra family reduced drastically.

"Then, a couple of months after Rishi returned home, we lost Debraj to a massive heart attack. Of course, I've always had very nice people in my life, be it a loving family or friends. But even among them, I'd always be grateful to Suchita, for it she who took extra efforts to console me. She'd come and see me to ensure that I had company. That I was not wallowing in my grief. And god knows that if not for her, even the façade of strength I maintained during that time would have come crumbling down. I was at a very vulnerable phase in life—over 50 years old, and with nothing to fall back on other than the one thing I had lost just then, my best friend who was my husband.

"Rishi and Simran were shattered at Debraj's death too. But Simran was about 25 years old by then, and Rishi, 23 years old. Rishi had joined Sidhhanth's business, and Simran had set up her own fashion store. Her business began to flourish soon, and the Malhotras redid the outhouse in their lawn to make it her boutique. Rishi also helped Simran market her merchandise. Soon, from supplying her collection to the bigger stores in the city, Simran grew into having exclusive clients who visited her boutique by invitation—many of whom were foreigners.

"But something interesting was happening too. After Debraj's death, my gift to communicate with metaphysical entities sharpened. I don't know how but I remember the frequent dreams that woke me up at midnight, warning me of problems that were set to come. One day, a little terrified that I might be looked upon as a loony, I decided to confess to Suchita about my 'powers'. She simply embraced it as a part of me, and encouraged me to hone it further.

"I began studying about it a little more, reading books and interpreting more events. When I began reading events a little better, warning her and her dear ones of impending calamities, or calling out to them about joyous events coming their way, she began bringing some of her closest friends and family to me.

"Then one day, I remember walking into Simran's boutique and foreseeing a very important collaboration coming her way. Two days later, she came home to tell me of a clothes design contract she had won with Macy's store in Brooklyn.

"Soon, I began being known in certain parts of society for my gifts, but because I wasn't doing it for the money, I was very choosy whom I picked for the reading. Of course, Suchita was my filter. But all the excitement from reading, and reading correctly, and all the accolades coming my way slowly helped me get over the misery of losing the one support system I thought I had. Of course, I missed Debraj, but the pain was much lesser. I still look back upon those days and know it was only because of Suchita and her loving family that I made it through."

Poornima's narration had eased everyone into the story she told. Nisha had a smile on her face when Poornima mentioned Suchita, for she could almost place her as warm as the Sujata she had come to know.

Poornima went on. "But the Malhotra family would begin experiencing tragedies soon—one after another. And despite all my gifts, I would miss the signs," she said, running her hand to wipe out a tear, her voice choking. The change in her tone caught the others' attention, and they were now looking at her.

"The first of it was in early 2008, when while returning late night from an office meeting, Sidhhanth and Rishi were instantly killed by a drunken driver who had lost control of his speeding car and had veered into theirs," Poornima added.

The room was deathly quiet now, Poornima's narration taking each of them through a range of emotions. Yet, at the mention of the year, Akhil had suddenly looked away from Poornima and at his wife. "Wasn't that around the same time you had your surgery too, Ishu?" he asked her. Nisha looked up at him from where she had nestled her head on his chest, nodded in agreement, and went back to resting her head on him.

Poornima was carrying on with her story. "Sidhhanth and Rishi's death left Suchita and Simran devastated. But for me, in addition to losing someone who was almost my son too, the misery was multi-fold also because despite my gifts to 'see', I hadn't seen this coming. No dreams, no warnings, nothing. The guilt was corroding me from within especially given how Suchita had helped me get to where I was through my gifts.

"Yet, the determined souls that they were, neither Suchita nor Simran ever once questioned me about it. They simply carried on relentlessly, Simran with her boutique and Suchita with the uptake of property and all the acreage surrounding it. But my guilt cocooned me in parts, and I dropped by only once in a while to check if she needed anything. She carried on like the rock she was, with her tiny circle of support system. There was Hari *chacha*[10], the cook and cleaner; Pradeep, the one-man-army as we called him, to man the gates; and her dear sister Nina who used to come visiting from Pune once in a while to check on the mother–daughter duo. Nina had returned from France after she'd heard about Sidhhanth and Rishi. In time, Suchita and her daughter were beginning to cope with all that was happening in their lives; they were getting back with their lives. Still steeped in guilt, I remained on the periphery of their lives. And yet, even as everything began seeming like it was falling in place for them, fate had other plans."

Now, Poornima stopped speaking. She was trying hard to control her emotions, and her eyes were welling up. She ran a quick finger to clear a tear drop threatening to roll out of the corner of her eye.

Then she took a long deep breath and like she was trying to drown the memory of something she may have had a hand in, she went on. "On the morning of 28th March 2013, everyone in the house was found murdered all over the house and boutique." The latest piece in the narrative had the whole listening party sitting upright!

"Nina had been visiting then, and was planning to return to Pune that evening. Also found among the dead bodies was Jignesh's body, with a bullet to his forehead. Some say he'd pulled the trigger on himself. But nothing has yet been understood about what happened that day. Needless to say, I am unable to forgive myself. For having let my guilt take me over during their bad times, after everything Suchita had done to get out of mine. For not letting myself read the signs of the tragedy that awaited them. About losing almost everything I called my own. About losing my family.

"Oh and what a beastly sight it was that I walked into! Blood everywhere—on the floors, the walls, the carpets, and the flower pots. I remember walking into the boutique, the otherwise fresh sandalwood fragrances in the room was taken over by the stench of drying blood and rotting flesh. My foot had even slipped on something sticky. It took me a little to understand it was blood I had stepped on. I remember seeing Simran's beautiful collection of stoles on the counter that day, all of it soaked in blood. Her stoles were her pride. To watch those washed in blood left me almost powerless.

"You know, I hadn't felt as bereft as that even when Debraj left me. Despite all that I had with Debraj, it felt like it was with Suchita that I had grown. I had come to imagine I wouldn't lose it—lose her. That day, as I watched the police clean the blood and limbs off the place, I remember realising how lonely I had become. I had lost everything when Suchita and Simran were butchered!" Poornima said, sobbing with her face hidden in her hands, shaking uncontrollably at the trauma the memory brought back.

Not a dry eye remained in the gathering. Nisha, who was close to tears listening to the whole story, broke down too.

It was Om Prakash who walked up to Poornima's side, trying to console her. But Poornima shook him away gently, apologizing softly. One could see she was trying to gather herself again. Then when she was back in control and her body upright, she wiped her tears away. "Despite all the gifts I was blessed with, I hadn't seen ghastly crime coming their way. I decided to stop the readings. If it couldn't save my family, what good was any of it?"

No one said anything. Nisha shifted, snuggling closer to Akhil, and he held her tighter. Om Prakash stood by Poornima's side looking distraught. And Ankit remained seated on the sofa, with his forehead resting on his palms joined as if in salutation.

"But then, when recently, up on hearing your help Ramya's screams the day she was attacked—I was in my garden picking out flowers for my puja. I had never heard a scream as piercing as that. Then I saw you and Akhil drive out of your gates soon after, with her in the backseat of your car. And just like that, despite me, it all came crowding back—that gift, as Om Prakash calls it, the one I tried to ignore after Siddhant and Rishi had died. And I knew there was an onslaught of something beginning here," she said, a tired smile showing on her face as she looked at Om Prakash.

"When anyone dies, unless their bodies are sanctified, the spirits, good or evil, remain trapped in that medium, waiting to satiate its will on unassuming victims. But the agents attached to the property had made a rushed sale to cover up the menace that had affected the property, without sanctifying the property."

The atmosphere in the room was tense and everyone was quiet now. It was Om Prakash who spoke next. "With Ramya's incident, Poornima *ji* reached out to me because we had worked together before. And since then, we have been conducting pujas between us and chanting mantras in the attempt to rid effects of the spirit."

"Ah! So that's what you used to do," said Nisha, a glimmer of understanding lighting up her eyes. And then scrunching her nose while grinning guiltily, she added, "I used to watch you, you know, from my bedroom window, wondering if you were up to any good."

The innocence in her assumption suddenly lightened the solemn mood in the room for a few seconds, and everyone laughed, and Akhil held her a little closer.

Chapter 17

When the room settled back, Ankit pitched in, "It has been over five years since the incident Poornima *ji* just mentioned, and though the incident took place before I was stationed here, I know my predecessors have tried everything to crack the case. We haven't really yet had a breakthrough in the case. Of course, there are assumptions and rumours. But they are all considered circumstantial. So when Nisha's brother Roni told me about your interest in buying the property, Nisha, I was compelled to warn you. You do remember, don't you?"

Nisha nodded at the memory. "But I was drawn to this property, Ankit," she said looking at him and then turning her glance at Akhil, her voice tinged with a slight guilt.

"Yes, I remember Roni telling me that too. And when Akhil called me earlier this evening, telling me about bizarre happenings that took place, my heart sank a little, but for some reason, I also believed that things were finally falling in place, and that we might actually solve this murder mystery," replied Ankit. "So, Akhil, when you called, I was almost certain there was more than just a break in here. I was just hoping Nisha and you were fine."

"But..." Nisha started and then stalled, and then continued. "I want to know why the spirit is attacking me. I haven't done anything to anyone."

Om Prakash replied, "An explanation could be a little complicated. By what has been happening to Nisha in these past few days and the apparitions of Suchita that appear only to Nisha, I am beginning to believe that Nisha has rattled the spirit somehow. And Suchita is trying to caution her about it. But what is Suchita's connection here? And why Nisha? Understanding that might be the first step to unravel this puzzle."

Poornima was silent through all this. And then she looked up at Nisha and said, "You mentioned you had a surgery around Rishi and his dad's accident. What was that about?"

"I had gone out with my friends and was returning home when I simply slumped and fell on the roadside," Nisha explained. "My friends rushed me to a hospital, and the doctors there discovered that I had a serious heart dysfunction called cardiomyopathy. I needed an emergency cadaveric transplant and was lucky because they found an organ donor in that very hospital I was taken to, and the donor was a perfect match for me."

Poornima was looking straight into Nisha's eyes. "And when did this take place?"

"25th of January 2008," Nisha replied without thinking. And then seeing the look on Poornima's face, she stopped, looking slightly shocked at Poornima and Om Prakash's steady gaze at her. Then she asked, "When had the accident that killed Rishi and his dad taken place?"

"25th of January 2008," replied Poornima slowly. She wrapped her arms around herself, as if to ward off a chill that had suddenly set in. And she noticed that everyone in the room was affected just as she was. They were all looking at each other.

Then Om Prakash began his voice barely audible to the rest, "Could it be...?"

"No, no, the donor's name was not Rishi," said Nisha, catching on. "In fact, I had even wanted to contact the donor family, but I was told that they didn't want to because it was too painful for them. I respected their wishes and let it be. But I shall never forget that name—it had given me back the gift of life. His name was Rushabananda Malhotra."

"Yes, Rushabananda Malhotra, also called Rishi Malhotra for short," stated Poornima matter-of-factly. "Rushabananda was the name of his grandfather, which became his official name too. But he was Rishi to family and friends."

But before the significance of the news could sink into Nisha, Poornima continued, an urgency seeping into her voice. "Now, think hard, both of you...is there an important occasion coming up for either of you?"

Nisha and Akhil looked at each other and shrugged their shoulders. "Nothing I can think of," said Akhil.

"Me neither. But that being said, I can hardly remember any dates, other than that of my monthly cycles," said Nisha with a chuckle, and then her face drained off any expression. She turned around to look at Akhil, and when their eyes met, Akhil knew.

"Could you...are you pregnant?" he asked her, his voice trembling slightly with a mix of excitement and trepidation at what that could mean for them.

Instead of responding to the question, Nisha simply ran up the stairs to the bedroom to grab one of her pregnancy kits. Akhil ran right behind her.

Even as the couple were off in their bedroom, the living room was so thick with anticipation you could cut through it with a knife! A minute later they heard

Nisha delighted screams and Akhil's laughter.

But in the living room, the mood was mostly sombre. The three of them there had turned towards the noise. "Ah! This could be why," said a suddenly haggard-looking Om Prakash.

Poornima knew what he meant, and she was looking back at him worriedly. Ankit, on the other hand, was between beaming, waiting to join in Nisha and Akhil's celebrations, and confused, wondering what Om Prakash had meant. "Why are you two looking like you so morose? Isn't this good news?" he asked.

"*That*'s the important occasion, Ankit," said Om Prakash. But Ankit kept looking back at him quizzically. He wasn't following.

And before Om Prakash could start explaining, the husband–wife duo came down the stairs to share the good news with the rest of them.

"Congratulations, dear girl," said Poornima with a smile that was not reaching her eyes. "I hope this news brings you all the joy you have wished for in life."

Nisha and Akhil exchanged glances. They had caught a note they had not expected to in Poornima's voice.

"Is there a problem?" asked Akhil imagining something else had come up.

But Om Prakash had pulled out a paper from his coat's pockets, and began drawing astrological charts where he sat, all the while murmuring something that sounded like he was adding or multiplying something. He hadn't heard Akhil's question. Instead, he spoke to Nisha.

"Give me your day, date, and time of birth. And I hope you remember the place of your birth too," he said rather matter-of-factly as he continued drawing out the chart.

"14th November 1990," replied Nisha, looking one after another at Akhil and Om Prakash. The joy of her recent discovery was wiped out of her face. Poornima had moved closer to Om Prakash, standing by, eagerly waiting to hear what he was learning through the charts.

Chapter 18

It was past 11.00 PM, and one by one, the party in the living room realised they hadn't had any dinner. Akhil called for food from one of the couple's favourite restaurants nearby.

While they waited for their food to arrive, Om Prakash began explaining to them what he had learnt through his charts. "According to your planetary positions when you were born, you were not supposed to outlive that heart dysfunction," he said to a now visibly shaken Nisha.

On seeing her in that state, Akhil instinctively walked up to her and put his arm around her. She looked up at him, bewildered.

"Two life events intersected that day," Om Prakash was going on. "One was death, which was to be yours, and the other—life. A saviour angel protected you this once and helped you stay alive when Rishi's organ was transplanted in you."

To the US-born-and-educated Akhil, the spiritual talk was sounding beyond ridiculous, but there was something about the way his wife paid heed to it that stopped him from mocking what was happening before him.

"And there is only way of finding out if any of this is true," said Om Prakash. "By contacting a closed dead relative of the diseased whose soul has moved into your body; in other words, by communicating with Suchita's ghost."

And despite Nisha's eagerness, Akhil couldn't hold back his anger at the inexplicable logic of all that was being spoken. "I am sorry, but I think I am unable to stand around and watch any of this anymore," he said, a little sneer lining his lips. "I mean...who in their right mind believes in ghosts? And even if one did, how would you 'communicate' with one?"

It was Poornima who spoke this time. "I understand your scepticism, Akhil. But please understand that ghosts, the paranormal, and spirits are words that have accompanied many stories for ages. The existence of paranormal elements, even though not supported by many, is believed by many others too, and this is despite the fact that not all of those who believe in these have had such experiences nor have adequate evidences to prove it. We believe in God, don't we, even when we haven't seen God or experienced that existence? And like every action has an equal and opposite reaction, a belief in God necessitates the presence of evil. And that could move beyond religion, literature, mythology, fiction, occultism, and folklore—usually settling in each of our hearts."

Suddenly, there was a loud ringing, and everyone suddenly turned their heads in the direction of the noise. It was Salim at the intercom, announcing the arrival of their dinner. Om Prakash collected the takeaway, and headed into the kitchen with Nisha to serve up the food into bowls and containers. With the aroma of the food wafting in, everyone suddenly realised how hungry they were and began to hurriedly dig into the food.

After the food was cleared off, they sat around Poornima as she explained how good and evil souls try to possess a body so that it can carry out their bidding. Then she added, "It is clear that there is a spirit targeting you, Nisha. And given how she's been making her appearances, I am almost certain Suchita is trying to ward it off from you. She's probably trying to save her son Rishi's soul in Nisha from being captured by the evil spirit. If she could save Nisha, she would save her dead son's soul too," Poornima said.

"And there may be a connection between Suchita and everyone's death from back then, and the spirit that's trying to attack Nisha," Poornima mused. "So the only way to crack this is to let the apparition come back to you and explain what she knows."

For the first time since the day's events, Nisha felt a chill run up through her spine at the mention of meeting Sujata again. She was not that warm woman she had known in these last few days. She was an apparition. A ghost. The spirit of a woman who was trying to safeguard her son's spirit. And that changed everything. At least to the point that Nisha knew she was not dealing with someone in the earthly realm. Poornima could gauge her discomfort and she walked up to her and tried to comfort her. Nisha and Poornima spoke to each other for a little longer until they realised it was close to 1.00 in the morning. And the party of five split up.

Ankit got up and offered to drop both Poornima and Om Prakash at Poornima's home as he headed back home too. Nisha and Akhil locked up after them and headed to their bedroom, hoping they could cuddle up into well-deserved and restful sleep.

No sooner had they hit their heads on the pillow than they were fast asleep.

Chapter 19

It was about 4.00 AM when Nisha woke up with an urgent need to pee. She used the washroom, washed her hands, and stepped out. And there, in the reflection of the moonlight, she saw the hazy apparition of who she had known briefly as Sujata, standing at the window, looking outside. Now, despite her trepidations earlier that night, Nisha walked up to her knowing that she was looking at a ghost, and sat next to where she stood.

"So you know who I am," said Suchita, turning around and looking at Nisha.

"Yes, I do. But that doesn't stop me from liking you as I did before I knew who you were, although I admit it scared me to think that I might have to confront you again," replied Nisha.

Suchita's apparition looked back at her and smiled. "Do you know? Everything Poornima said was right. We did have a beautiful life—Sidhhanth, Rishi, Simran, and I. And Poornima and I shared a bond only sisters do. I just know it all came crumbling down, and there was nothing I could do to stop it. And that poor woman blamed herself so much. I knew she was keeping away because she couldn't face her guilt about missing the signs of the fatal accident. I had hoped she'd return from her mental lockout and know I wouldn't ever hold it against her. How could I? But she was broken and bound in guilt like I hadn't imagined. I wish I had worked a little more to get her out of it," the apparition said.

"But anyway, now, it's time to stop this evil from ruining what's remaining of my family through you. And I know I have the power to do it," she said.

"How do you mean?" Nisha asked, wondering if what Poornima and Om Prakash had deduced correctly.

"Nisha, the child you conceived carries my son's soul," replied Suchita, reading her mind and confirming her doubts. "And the only way the spirit will accomplish its evil desires is by trying to seize and destroying you. It needs to kill you and your unborn child to satiate his mad vengeance—to destroy my family in its entirety."

"But why? I just don't understand. Who is this trying to hurt me? I mean, I know I haven't done anyone any harm, and from what Poornima *ji* tells me, neither have you or your family members. Then why is this spirit trying to hurt you and your loved ones...? And now, my baby...what is driving it so? What could you or any one in your family have done to it?" Nisha blurted unable to hold back her curiosity any longer.

Suchita's apparition remained quiet for a moment. Then, looking outside the window towards the boutique, she said, "I was there, you know, when it all happened. In my daughter's boutique—where everything in my life had been stolen brutally, and cut up into bloody pieces," Suchita continued. "You ask me who killed my family. It was one of our own—our dear friend once upon a time—Jignesh—avenging what he lost, he said."

Nisha couldn't believe what she was hearing. Wasn't Jignesh that man from the picture, who seemed so shy, who had been a dear friend of the family...? He'd a son too...one who had feelings for Simran, Suchita's daughter.... What was he avenging? Nisha was unable to comprehend what could have changed it all for him. And even as she sat wondering about it all, she could hear Sujata's voice in her ears.

"You see, some years before Siddhant's death, Jignesh and Sidhhant had made a pact to enter the garment industry," Sujata began saying. "The investment was close to INR 200 crores. Siddhanth didn't have sufficient funds at that time, so Jignesh, his fundraising manager, was asked to raise funds from the market and the get ahead with the plan of action. The documentation around the agreement, which was that Siddhanth would pay 50 per cent of the investment amount from our property, was awaiting finalization. Jignesh had already begun raising the funds from the market.

"But even as the agreement papers were getting readied, Sidhhant and Rishi died in the accident. While it was the end of the world for Simran and me, Sidhhant's sudden death began a new chapter of ruin for Jignesh because Sidhhant had promised Jignesh a loan to pay back creditors for some of his failed businesses, none of which I had known about. There were no records of their pact. The pact was word-of-mouth.

"But back then, I hadn't realised the misery Jignesh was going through. He was a trusted business partner of Sidhhant, who was also a renowned businessman in the country. But Siddhanth's death came at a time when another of his business partners accused him of wrong doings; it had led to his arrest. That loss triggered a sense of helplessness in him that set off an irreversible chain of erroneous beliefs, which, given his circumstances then, led him into a satiating his losses criminally.

"I remember he had come to me telling me about the agreement with Sidhhant, but because Sidhhant hadn't discussed those business plans with me and because I thought I was in a vulnerable position after his death, I refused to give in to Jignesh's explanation when he told me about the agreement between them. For whatever reasons that led me to the decision back then, besides not willing to risk INR 100 crores, I decided to withdraw my share from the garment project. I went with Simran instead. I hadn't realised my actions had left Jignesh questioning my sense of loyalty towards his years of friendship. I hadn't known how betrayed he felt. I really didn't, you know!

"But the investment in Simran's business began bringing more returns, and those successes that snapped something in Jignesh. From then on, his life took a new turn towards doom. While on the one hand, he suffered the humiliation of not being able to repay the money to investors who had once taken business lessons from within the committed timeline, my vulnerabilities coupled with indecisions about his capabilities added to his need for vengeance.

"After a year, a junior partner filed a fraudulent case against him. Many others jumped the bandwagon with wrong allegations to take advantage of his situation. The trial went on for three years. It bankrupted him. Around then, citing irreconcilable differences that had cropped up in their marriage, even Radhika left him. The allegations, imprisonment, and the loss of his hard-earned reputation affected him severely, and left him a shell of his former self. He was psychologically shattered.

"Soon, he lost all the cases against him and was taken into custody. After Simran refused his Mehul's proposal for marriage, a heartbroken Mehul moved to the States. To add salt to injury, even I had moved on from my misery in life, not being associated with many things I used to be with when Sidhhant was alive. Perhaps the callousness in me is guilty of having developed the criminal in him."

Nisha had sat down listening to the story, as if almost watching a movie playing out, where the plot was incomprehensible, unfolding slowly and ever-changing.

"A spirit like that will do everything in its capacity to scare you, subjugate you," Sujata was saying. "But you need to be bold, my darling, and face that fear. Because every time evil smells fear, it grows a little more powerful, taking you a little more in its grip. Face your fears, my girl, and have faith in me. I shall not let anything happen to you. I promise you that."

And just like that, there was nothing remaining of the apparition in the bedroom. Nisha simply sat there wondering about all that she'd heard.

Soon, as if following a cue, she found herself being led away from the room, leaving a sleeping Akhil in the room. She walked down the stairs, opened the door, and stepped on the stone-pathway that led to the entrance of the boutique. It was still dark outside, but Nisha kept walking towards the room as if unable to stoop herself. She could sense that she was no longer in charge of her body. But as she walked to the boutique, she noticed that the lights were switched on, and there was someone inside. It was a tall, young woman, standing by one of the corner shelves, humming a melodious tune. The humming was accompanied by the soft clinking sounds of her silver bangles.

In her other hand was a beautiful red shiny stole dancing in a breeze that was blowing around her. The stole was very lovely, soft to the touch. Nisha had never seen that stole before. As she stepped towards the figure and the stole, she heard someone call her name. "Nisssha....aaaa," it whispered. Nisha was on the edge.

Now, despite being aware of her fear Nisha, walked towards the woman. She stood there, knowing she was staring at the back of a slender woman with long, straight hair, dressed in one of those elegant clothes that stood out in its simplicity. She had worn big loopy ear rings, and she was using her right hand to tuck in strands of her long silky hair behind her ears. Then, she turned around to face Nisha, and that's when Nisha saw the disfigured face. Blood was oozing through tiny punctures on wounds caused by the impact of a blunt object.

Nisha screamed, but her voice wouldn't come out. Then she realised it was the other woman who was screaming. Nisha turned around to run. But just then a black shadow, as dark as a raven, approached her. *Every time it smells fear, it grows a little more powerful, taking you a little more in its grip,* Nisha remembered Suchita's apparition telling her.

But that was not helping Nisha conquer her fear just then. That's when she saw Suchita standing inside the boutique. There was a suitcase lying next to her, with the clothes in it strewn all over the boutique floor. Just then, she noticed blood on the boutique floor. It was oozing out of Suchita's chest, where an axe lay pierced into her.

"Stop it," Suchita was screaming. "Why are you doing this?"

But all Nisha could see was a hand that came of out nowhere, slashing Suchita again with the bloodied axe. The axe fell on her neck next. Suchita was screaming, her cries ringing through Nisha's bones. And then there was the black apparition again. Now it was before her, turning towards her. She could see its face now, under the black hat it had on itself. It was indeed that man from Poornima's picture, the one she knew as Jignesh: a man who just now seemed to look very unlike the warm person who seemed to have been smiling shyly in that picture.

Now Nisha began screaming, her voice drowning the screams of the other women in the room. She ran out of the boutique towards Salim sitting in his cubicle at the gate, but none of the commotion seemed to have reached him. He seemed to be writing something in the log book, with his head bent over. Nisha was screaming as she ran towards the gate, but Salim didn't look up still. Soon she reached the cubicle and screamed out to Salim to help. He simply lifted his head to look up at her and she could see that it was not Salim looking back at her. It was that man again, smiling at her, a cynical madness gleaming through his eyes. "You can't hide, Rishi," was all he said.

****

Nisha was still screaming. But she was on her bed and Akhil was next to her. Her screams had woken up Akhil, and he was trying to calm her. "He'll kill me," Nisha was crying loudly now. "He'll kill our baby. My baby!"

"Shhh...sshh, darling," said a slightly disoriented but now fully awake Akhil, as he held his wife in his arms, trying to calm her. "You just had a bad dream, baby. It's been a few crazy days, I know. But this was just a dream, baby, nothing else...just a bad dream. I promise. Shhhh...my love, shhhush, my baby..." he kept repeating, rocking her body as she pushed against his chest.

But Nisha was inconsolable, crying about a man she'd seen...screaming on about him coming to kill Suchita and Simran. "I know what happened in this house all those years ago. Sujata told me what happened. I saw it. I almost saw it all, Akhil. Oh, how he butchered them. Oh no! Why? Why did he have to? Now he wants to kill me. My baby. He wants to kill us," Nisha kept repeating, her sobs uncontrollable.

And as he tried to calm her, Akhil quickly grabbed his phone from the nightstand and dialled the number Poornima had shared the previous night in case he wanted to get in touch with her. It was close to 4.30 AM now; the street lights were still on outside, their warm luminescence lighting up the darkness of the early morning hours. The phone rang a couple of times on the other side before Poornima answered. He didn't need to speak a word but at the other end of the phone, Poornima could hear Nisha's screams and sobs. "I'll get there right away," she said as she cut the call.

Chapter 20

Akhil let Poornima and Om Prakash in through the door. "She says she saw someone and what happened all those years ago, but I think it was all just a nightmare," Akhil was speaking hurriedly as they all ran up the stairs to get to her.

Poornima entered the bedroom and noticed that the clothes that were lying strewn on the floor the previous night were now all gone, and the wardrobe was shut, most likely rearranged.

But Nisha was sitting up on the bed, looking like she had seen a ghost. And Poornima was certain she had.

"*Beta*, it's okay," she said, rushing to Nisha's side.

"No, I saw it. I saw them getting murdered," Nisha was saying, crying like a little child. "He killed them. It was him. The man in the picture you had shown me yesterday. He killed them all. I saw him killing them. Oh god, he axed them to death, Poornima. Why? Why?"

Poornima and Akhil exchanged urgent glances.

"I think she means Jignesh," said Poornima then, looking at Om Prakash who was standing by the bed. "She must have been led into the memories of what happened here."

"Yes, it seems like it's his spirit," agreed Om Prakash solemnly.

****

When she woke up next, it was still dark, and Akhil was sitting next to her. She held out her hand to touch his waist, but the moment she did that, his skin felt soft and silky as a fabric. Now she realised Akhil was not in the pyjamas he had on; instead, he was in a soft silk pink saree.

She managed to half open her sleepy eyes and asked, "Why are you in a saree, Akhil?"

But he simply turned around and said, "Please don't kill her. Please leave her alone. That's my son."

Nisha looked back in shock at the figure beside her, for Akhil was now a woman with Suchita's face, begging her not to kill. Nisha screamed in fear and fell out of bed on her hand, hitting and hurting her elbows in the process. As she rubbed the hurt on her elbows, Suchita's urgent pleas rang in her ears, "Run away, Rishi! Nisha, take him away. Jignesh has gone mad."

Then again, Nisha could hear Suchita begging again. "Don't kill her. Please don't kill her, Jignesh. I will give you everything you ask for."

Nisha was getting up to run, and though her body was hurting all over, she was being prodded towards the kitchen. As she got closer, she could smell something foul in the air, the stench growing more intense as she entered the kitchen. She followed the stench into a corner. And she pulled out a bin from under one of the shelves. It was stuffed with bloody limbs.

Nisha screamed and ran out of the kitchen into the living room where she tripped on something and fell to the ground, her hand hitting some warm, sticky liquid. She realised she'd had fallen over a body lying on the floor. She looked up to see the dead body of a woman; with an imprint of pure fear on her face. Nisha hadn't known the woman but she heard a voice crying, "Nina! Noooooooo!! No! No! What has he done to you?" It was Suchita's voice, but Nisha knew Suchita was not around—she was dead. And yet, the voice was coming through her.

Nisha struggled to get up and run, but instead, her hand slipped on the sticky liquid and she fell forward, hitting the ottoman sitting close by. But sitting in a pile near the ottoman was a bunch of limbs, their gory flesh and blood trickling all over the place. Among the pile was a cut head of someone Nisha hadn't known either, but somewhere within her, she knew that it was of someone Suchita had known. "Oh, Bahadur, my trusted boy! Oh why him? Why, Jignesh? Why him? He was just the driver. How did he bother you? Why...?" she was wailing loudly now, her heart pounding like it was going to fall off. And Nisha understood that she was one with Suchita now, experiencing everything the older woman had seen and felt on that horror-torn day when she watched her near and dear ones getting butchered by a mad man.

"Why?" she heard a voice asking. "Why, you ask?" And then the room bellowed with hysterical, sinister laughter.

Nisha could make out the silhouette of a man dressed in a dark outfit from head to toe. On his head was a black hat, and over his shoulder was a bloody axe.

"Jignesh, why are you doing this to me?" Suchita was still talking to the man through Nisha. "Sidhhant trusted you. I trusted you as my own brother. And you loved this family so much. Why are you creating this mayhem? Killing all these innocent people one by one?"

"Of course, I loved your family as my own, but where were you when I was sinking? When I lost my honour, and everything I held close to my heart? When I came to you to help me? So I avenged. This is my revenge. When I was alive and lost everything, no one wanted anything to do with me. After my death, there won't be anything of mine left behind, no one to even cry for me. So I choose to remain alive in people's mind as a black fear. And every time I commit a brutal murder, I shall be remembered, and thus revived.

"Yes, oh dear Suchita, this is my vengeance, for everything I couldn't get back from you. Because what began with you, I shall end with all yours."

He lifted his blood-soaked axe at Nisha. She screamed for help, but no one heard her. Jignesh ran his axe at her shoulder, and the pain that ran through her made her scream out even louder. Blood was spilling everywhere. He then lifted Nisha and propped her on his shoulder, carrying her to the storeroom in the backyard. There, he put her down on the ground.

Nisha could felt the blood squirting onto the walls of the room through the fresh wounds inflicted on Suchita's body. She was rapidly losing consciousness. Watching through Suchita's sub-consciousness, Nisha was looking back at the beautiful days that she spent with her loving family in the house, the laughter and joy with all her dear ones including Jignesh and his wife Radhika, and Mehul, their adorable and loving son who was in love with Simran. How could it all have gone so wrong? And turn Jignesh, the man who would do anything for his friend and her husband Sidhhant, who loved her kids as his own, to such a blood-thirsty demon? But Suchita's eyes were shutting now, and so Nisha's, whose body's auto-mechanism was shutting it down to avoid the intense pain running through her limbs. Nisha could sense death, her heartbeat slowing down.

Her eyes were shutting now, visuals blurring. Nisha was watching Suchita dying before her. She could feel her eyes closing, the most profound and deepest nap of her life settling in, carrying her far away from earthly pleasures.

But just then she felt her body jerk. "No, no, don't let her shut her eyes," Nisha could hear around her. *Was it Poornima speaking? Yes, that was her.* And then she heard Akhil's voice, "Wake up, darling. Wake up. I am not going to let anything happen to you, my love," he said.

There were the sounds of rhythmic chanting that rang through the room:

"Om!"

"Vidya raakshasastapishthaih[11]*,*

"dahashaso raakshaso pahyasaman[12]

"Parah astu"[13]

Maa no reksho."[14]

The chanting went on.

Nisha was coming around; she opened her eyes slowly, the blurry images around her clearing up only to realise she was lying in Akhil's arms. She could see Poornima on her side too, and Ankit, standing beside Poornima.

Had I been merely asleep? She wondered. *Was this all just a nightmare?* It had felt like a terrible journey from her death to reality. *But everything was so life-like. Suchita! Oh the pain she went through during her dying moments*, she thought and began weeping like a child. Poornima was now with Nisha, cradling her in her arms, even as Akhil stood by unable to control his emotions watching his dear wife in such a disoriented state.

It was all a horrible nightmare. She was alive and well, Nisha realised, and she was near the love of her life Akhil, but she had seen from up close the misery that had been inflicted upon a loving family, a woman and her loved ones. She was not able to control herself, and she was crying out loud for all that was lost in that house, lost to a loving woman. And that by a man they had all trusted and loved!

She could make out Om Prakash's voice in the background, repeatedly chanting his mantras. Poornima and Akhil were near her.

But a little beyond, near her favourite seat at the French windows, was the silhouette of Suchita, looking out of the window, at the boutique. Her face was soaked in the sorrow Nisha had just experienced through the nightmare.

Suchita was now looking back at her from the window, her face racked in pain. And Nisha understood why she was experiencing any of this.

"Please save my son's soul before this mad man tries to kill him. Please," she was pleading. "Don't let him grow stronger. Please capture the spirit and bring him solace in fire."

Chapter 21

It was close to daybreak, and the four of them were standing near the boutique now. "The news of Siddhanth's car accident was a shock to all of us," the apparition of Suchita was speaking through a now calm Nisha. "But it was only on that ghastly night of slaughter and murder that I learned how his death had also left Jignesh exposed to creditors whom he owed money to. I hadn't until then understood the intensity of the pain Jignesh carried in him, which was transforming into a cold hatred for anyone around him.

"On the night of 24th, Simran was to head to London for a meeting, and I was to drop her at the airport. I remember talking to Simran even the previous day about Mehul, asking if she had reconsidered Mehul's proposal for marriage. She had told me that she couldn't consider Mehul for marriage given how she had come to see him as a brother. And I let the matter be.

"But that was the night the slaughters began, when we were just getting ready to leave for the airport. But even though he came for me, Jignesh was intercepted by Bahadur, my guard. He committed his first murder by killing Bahadur; he cut up the body and shoddily left it in plastic bags in the kitchen. And with that, his already deranged mind had found pleasure in killing. Soon, he was on a spree, murdering anyone he thought was associated with me, including my loving sister Nina—Nina, who had nothing to do in any of this...who was simply in the wrong place at the wrong time! And then when he was sure he had killed the last of my close family, he turned the gun on himself. So many died in this house because of a mentally unstable man whose internal demons I may have fanned into transforming him too. My guilt of perhaps having a hand in his fall drew out my energies from stopping him, until I knew he was targeting you because you were carrying my son."

Everyone was quiet now, looking on even as Suchita's apparition began to fade. "For a man who left so much destruction in his wake, it would be difficult for anyone to forgive him," she was saying, her voice getting softer and less audible as moments passed. "But unless he is forgiven, his soul would always remain in the nether world, seeking more and more vengeance. Release him please. Please offer a prayer for him. I made mistakes of not looking beyond my pain. And as deep as my distress may have been, it created a monster in him. Forgive him. Please. Forgive me."

****

The innocuous-looking day wore on, a light breeze blowing outside. Four people sat in front of the boutique at the Treehouse Estate. Om Prakash had created a small pit where he had set up a little fire and was silently reciting his mantras, his eyes shut tightly and one arm stretched as in offering. Nisha sat close to Akhil, facing Om Prakash. Poornima sat close, too, meditating to make the evil spirit appear.

The four had heeded to Suchita's advice and were conducting rituals for all the deceased in the house, so as to release their souls. And among the rituals was one set aside for the spirit of Jignesh, to help him be at peace with his doings and seek retribution despite the black fear he had let his sorrows grow him into.

THE END

[1] A shortened form of "Didi", which in Hindi means elder sister; the term is also used respectfully by younger people to address older girls/women

[2] "Allah is gracious!"

[3] A Hindi suffix used as a mark of respect when addressing someone.

[4] Tempering spices and condiments in oil or ghee; it is usually considered the last step to completing most Indian daals and dishes.

[5] Savoury fritters made of vegetables like potatoes, onions, and spinach dipped in the batter of ground Bengal gram, an Indian favourite relished especially with the evening tea/coffee

[6] "You like pakodas, don't you?"

[7] "Yes, we like them."

[8] "How are you Om *ji*?"

[9] "I am well. How about you?"

[10] An endearment meaning father's brother

[11] Pierce the demons with your sharpest arrows

[12] Burn the demons and protect us

[13] Destroy those demons who are troubling us day and night

[14] Let us be protected from the killer demons and also who cause discord among us.

Contents

Printed by Libri Plureos GmbH in Hamburg,
Germany